Life at the Pond

G.S. Chambers

Faith Jones, Illustrator

Life at the Pond is a work of fiction. Names, characters, places, and incidents either are the product of the author's imagination or are used fictitiously. Any resemblance to actual persons, living or dead, events, or locales is entirely coincidental.

Published in the United States of America by
Theophany Press
Bakersfield, CA
theophanypress.com

Illustrated by Faith Jones
Cover Design: Keith Silvas
Title Page/Break Image: ID 88577299 © Olena Melnyk | Dreamstime.com
Cattail/Birds Image: ID 25785781 © Oxygen64 | Dreamstime.com

ISBN 978-1-7339710-6-5
Library of Congress Control Number: 2020921916

This book and series is dedicated to my beloved father

Retired Major Philip R. Andrews (1924-2018)

He was my hero and my mentor. His first love was for the Lord, which I benefited from through his prayers. His second love was for the arts, both in painting and writing. He encouraged me to stick with writing through his critiques of chapters to the pencil drawings of the pond and surroundings. Thank you, Dad—your inspiration made it possible to reach my goal.

Contents

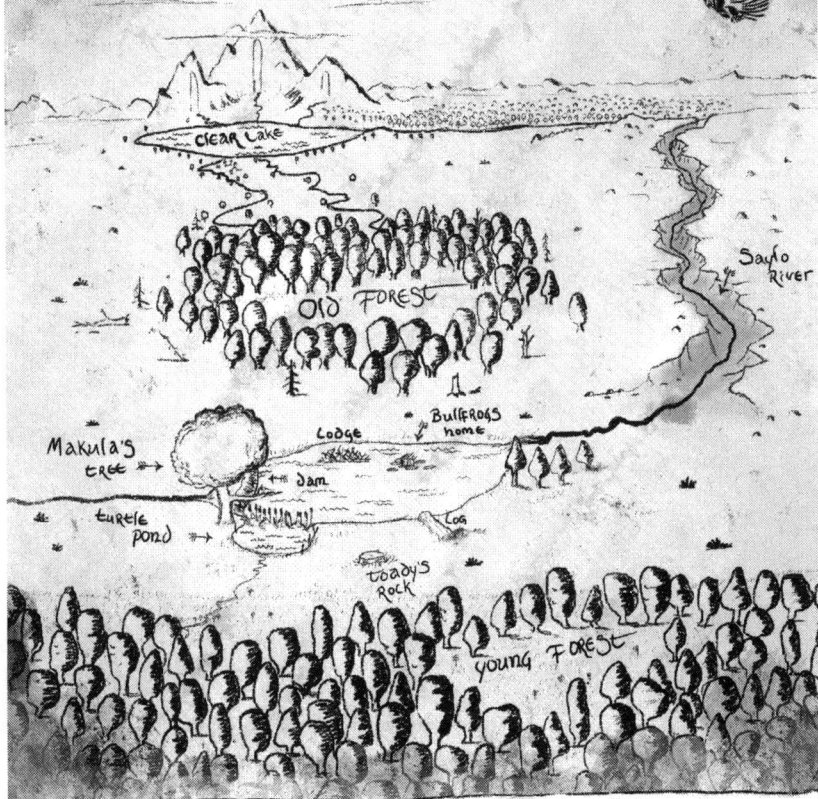

CHAPTER 1

Freddy and Seymour are best friends and frogs. Their first home had been a tiny little mud-hole under a large Oak tree. While searching for a home of their own, two beavers, Peanut and Honey, came across the friendly frogs and decided this was the place for them. They built a dam creating a big beautiful pond and as time passed, many creatures came to call it home, too.

A vast fire had burned its way down the mountainside, coming near to the pond. Even with that, they were grateful it hadn't touched their homes and community. Freddy felt terrible for the creatures living in the Old Forest who had to flee theirs.

This tragedy reminded everyone of the terrible flood last spring, when the river swept Seymour away and the squirrels had lost their homes. Ziggy and his friends weren't sure if any of their family had escaped. All winter the squirrel crew wondered and worried about their clan. Now since spring was here, three of the crew set out on a search.

Ziggy volunteered to watch over the homes of his three friends while they were on their journey.

He didn't select anyone to be in charge because he never considers himself to be the leader of the group. Pleased with the way the group voted on everything and no one's wishes were above another's, he assumed they felt the same way. Except one squirrel had other ideas.

I'll be the leader at last, Randall thought. *Since Ziggy is staying home, I'm the best one for the job. I just need to establish my rules before we leave tomorrow.*

Randall called Swish and Fluff over to where he was standing. He marched back and forth in front of them with his tail held high and fluffed out twice its size.

"Okay guys, I've a few rules. One, there won't be any voting. What I say goes. Two, you will call me sir when talking to me. Three, you will groom your tails every day. Four, because I'm the leader I will be out in front and I allow no one to pass me. Five, this is the most important one, I keep the first choice of any food," Randall chittered in a snobby voice.

Stunned, Swish and Fluff's mouths flopped open. Randall marched off to the base of his tree and scurried up to his hole. The two stared at each other.

"Who does he think he is? King of the crew? I'm not following those rules. Ziggy never treated us that way," Swish objected, as his tail swept back and forth.

Though he didn't want to fight with Randall, Fluff agreed. "Let's see how it goes."

"Okay, but if he keeps this up, we'll ditch him."

Fluff's tail fur stood out in every direction as he groaned. "I hope it doesn't come to that."

The squirrels had noticed a border of trees a short distance from their homes and planned to head that way. However, there was one massive problem. A sweeping grass covered meadow ran between their forest and it.

It wasn't the cleverest thing for squirrels to travel through a grassland. Trees were their defense. In a meadow, squirrels can be easy snacks for both beasts on the ground, or in the air. They knew they'd need to travel through it and hoped there'd be a narrow place to dash across.

The first day was an easy one, for they stayed in the tree line bordering the meadow. The food was plentiful and travel was smooth as they glided from one tree to the next. Swish and Fluff allowed Randall to carry on with his crazy ideas. Yet, the next day Randall decided it was time to cross the meadow.

"Why here?" Swish asked. "Farther ahead you can see it's narrower, and we'd be nearer to the other forest." He pointed down the way.

Randall realized Swish was right. But he wasn't backing off and giving them a chance to seize his leadership from him. *No way!*

"I gave an order," he barked, his tail giving a quick twitch.

"It's too dangerous to be out in the open," Swish argued.

"Rule number one, you will obey my orders. We're heading into the meadow."

He scampered down the tree and into the tall grass. The other two hesitated a moment, then followed with great caution. A few steps in, Swish froze, his heart beat faster as he listened to the alarming crunch and rustling sound as if a wounded animal thrashed about. Realizing it was Randall, Swishes heart slowed, and he continued to creep between the clumps of grass. He and Fluff followed a natural pathway heading toward the other side. The last thing he wanted was to give their position away to a squirrel-eating beast.

Up ahead, Randall chittered in a loud voice, "Come on guys, you're too slow."

Swish cringed. *Has he no fear of a beast finding him?* The sun darkened and Swish glanced up. Strength left his bones as a frightening shadow floated over them. Swish and Fluff curled up together into small balls of fur, and squeezed their eyes shut.

I wish my heart would slow down. I feel as if I'm twitching, Swish thought. But it wasn't his beating heart at all. It was Fluff's rapid, puffing breath causing Swishes fur to flutter. Fear kept its grip on them as they waited for the piercing of sharp talons. However, the shadow continued to the forest they headed toward.

Opening one eye, Swish searched the sky. Slowly, he raised his head. There was no sign of the shadow. The two uncurled and moved in a quick creeping crawl toward the nearest stalk of grass. They slumped down and took shuddered breaths.

"That scared me, and I don't want to experience it ever again. My heart hurts!" Swish whispered to Fluff.

"I feel sick. Can we sit for a bit until my stomach stops spinning?" Fluff moaned.

Swish noticed the sun on the horizon and then surveyed the forest they wanted to reach. He realized they might not make it before dark.

"Wish we could Fluff, but we need to keep moving, we aren't even halfway there. We probably will have to spend the night in here and I want to be closer to it."

It was torture to creep along because what they desired to do was run like the wind. A shadow crossed above them again, but this time Swish and Fluff slid into a clump of grass for cover.

"We must keep going, but move slow," Swish whispered.

Swish listened for Randall, making sure they weren't too close. *If a creature hears him, I don't want it to eat me too.*

Fluff's stomach ached. He hadn't had a decent meal since entering the meadow. They had finally caught up with Randall, who was scrounging around for something to eat. He had found a few seeds and tucked them into his cheeks. Off to one side, Fluff let out a little chirp.

"Check out what I found." A nut lay in his paw.

"Where did you find it?" Randall asked. "Were there more?"

Fluff showed them where he had found it, and the three scurried around searching for more. Not finding any, they gave up. Fluff rolled the nut around in his paw, searching for the right place to open it. His plan was to share with the others.

Randall faced Fluff, "I told you I claim first choice in any food we find. That nut's mine." He made a grab for it, at the same time Swish jumped between them. He glared at Randall. The stony gaze in Swish's eyes made Randall back up a step.

"I don't think so," Swish said. "Fluff found it and he'll decide what to do with it, not you. No one's taking it from him."

Randall's tail went straight up and stiffened.

"That's rule number five, now give it to me," Randall barked and dove around Swish again to snatch the nut.

Swish slid back in front of Randall, "I said no!"

He turned his back on Randall and faced Fluff. "Do you remember voting on his rules?"

Fluff shook his head.

"There will be no voting, that's rule number one. My rules are law," Randall whined.

Swish ignored him. "Fluff, what's your vote? I vote no! I won't follow them."

"Me either." Peeking around Swish, he glared at Randall. "Your rules are unfair. Ziggy shared everything with us and we had a vote. I don't remember choosing you as the leader either."

Swish faced Randall. "The vote is two to one."

With his tail straight up and fluffed out, he stomped away. *I'll show them.*

Fluff broke open the nut and gave a portion to Swish. He called out to ask if Randall wanted a piece, but he ignored the offer, keeping his back to them. Secretly Randall gnawed on the seeds he had found.

As the sun slipped below the horizon, the night predators woke up. It would be a terrible choice to keep moving through the meadow. The three squirrels slid into the middle of a big clump of grass to wait until morning.

With a piercing stare, Randall leaned in and whispered. "It's your fault we're still here. If you'd kept up, we'd be in those trees by now." He glanced at Swishes tail and continued, "You're a mess. You need to groom your tail."

Swish had had enough. Scared, tired, and mad, he fumed. "If we had stayed in the trees until the meadow narrowed, we wouldn't be here, so don't blame me. Also, I'll groom my tail when I want to and not because of your stupid rules."

Randall exploded on Swish. "I'll tell you when and how you hear me? This is my adventure and you'll do as I say!"

"I think creatures throughout the meadow can hear you right now." Swish turned his back and ignored him.

After a restless night, Randall came up with a plan and so did the other two squirrels. When morning came, Swish and Fluff were nowhere in sight.

"Go ahead and take off, it's just fine with me," Randall chittered aloud. "Now I don't need to worry about anyone except for myself." There was no one to refuse his leadership and no one to make him mad. Soon his situation became clear. He—was—alone!

I'll get even with them.

Chapter 2

After a few hours of sleepless worry, Swish whispered to Fluff, "The moon is giving us enough light I can see the shadows of the first group of trees. If we run like crazy, we can make it."

They crept away from Randall, and like two nutty squirrels they dashed away. When Fluff and Swish reached the trees, they both collapsed.

"I'm glad we're out of there," Swish sighed. "Let's find a safe place to sleep."

After placing distance between themselves and Randall, the two squirrels curled into fluffy balls and fell asleep.

When morning came, they took a better survey of their surroundings. This part of the forest didn't bear the nut trees their clan needed to survive through a winter. Disappointed, they continued the search. Scampering forward, they came across a small field of flowers and grasses separating them from the rest of the forest.

Swish scanned the area. "To reach those trees, we must cross over. What do you think?"

Agitated, Fluff's tailed twitched back and forth. "I hate meadows. I wish there was an easier way."

They sat and studied the small grassland. Nothing shifted in or around the clumps. Butterflies flitted from flower to flower, and everything seemed peaceful.

"I see nothing dangerous. Are you ready?" Swish asked.

"I guess."

They scampered across and leaped onto the nearest tree. The squirrels peered into the dark forest with trees jammed tight together. Sunlight couldn't peek in, and the only living plants were around the base of the trees. These didn't seem to need much light. They had tannish-white stems with puffy red rounded tops. White spots dotted the surface.

"This is when I wish Ziggy was here. He'd jump right in, but I'm a little scared," Swish groaned.

"Me too. Even though I have the jitters, we won't find anyone if we don't start checking this forest."

As they inspected the nearest branch to leap on to, a voice from above cautioned them, "I don't think that's a good idea." Swish and Fluff stiffened, and their bodies rooted to the spot like two furry statues. The voice continued, "I haven't spotted you in these parts, what're you doing here?"

Too scared, Swish didn't answer, and Fluff could only chirp.

"Come on out with it, I won't hurt you. If I were, I'd have done it by now."

Dumb, dumb, dumb, it would never catch Ziggy this way, Swish thought. Finally, Swish took a glance up and there sat a creature with gray fur and a long-striped tail. It had black rings around its eyes. *It's a raccoon.*

Swish found his voice, "We…we're searching for our family who might've come here to live. The flood last year wiped out our homes."

"This forest has had no visitors in a long time. Nothing to eat in there," he pointed into the darkness. "I don't live in there either. I live in these trees on the outer ring."

"Have you noticed any new squirrels in your part of the trees?"

"A group came by, well before winter. I warned them off too. I expect they went around that way," he pointed toward the meadow. "Don't know if they were your clan. Didn't ask, just warned them to stay out of this forest. It's not safe."

"Thank you for your advice," Swish said.

He and Fluff took off around the outer tree ring and observed oak trees in the distance. Hearing the skitter of clicking nails trailing them as they raced along, they knew it was Randall. He stayed way behind, but continued to follow them.

Up ahead they saw a grove of trees which ringed a small island of grass. A huge oak tree stood in the middle of the area. When they reached it, Swish and Fluff noticed several squirrels were racing along the limbs, playing tag. A bark of warning sounded and they all paused. Then a chittering explosion of "SWISH, FLUFF" came from all directions. Here were their family and friends.

Someone else yelled, "Hey! Randall's here too."

Swish and Fluff glanced back, and there sat Randall, appearing as arrogant as usual. Only a quick flick of his tail showed his anger.

The three squirrels stayed with their families for several days, catching up on all the news. Their friends wanted to know where they had spent the winter.

"We've found a place by a pond," Fluff explained. "There are loads of nut trees and we each have our own hole. Ziggy is with us, though he stayed behind to watch after our homes. Also, we've become good friends with the other creatures who live there."

Thrilled to hear Ziggy was safe, his family chittered with happiness. Now they could stop worrying about the four missing squirrels.

Randall sat listening to the conversations. In a self-absorbed mood, he didn't speak to anyone.

One squirrel whispered to Swish, "What's wrong with Randall?"

Swish shrugged.

"Have you come back to live with us?"

Swish and Fluff had already discussed this between themselves.

"No, but we'll be back to visit and I'm sure Ziggy will come soon," Swish said.

The next day, Swish and Fluff were saying goodbye to everyone when Randall showed up.

"I'm leading us home," he said while his tail twitched back and forth. "You had no right to leave me behind, putting me in danger. You will follow me or else."

Swish's tail stood straight up. "Or else what? What exactly are you threatening to do? Take away our food or tell us how to conduct ourselves? You've already tried those, and we showed you how we felt about it. This is the deal, you can come with us, with the exception you aren't in charge."

Randall sucked in his breath. "You can't order me around."

"Okay, let's vote since this is a major decision. I vote you can come only under the condition I stated. What is your vote Fluff?"

"I vote the same as Swish," Fluff announced.

"I vote no." Randall stomped his foot.

"Well, I guess you're on your own because it's two to one."

"Now wait a minute."

"Let me ask you a question. Why are you coming back? You aren't happy at the pond," Swish asked.

For a moment Randall examined his thoughts. "No, I'm not happy. But that's where my home is and nobody can boss me around as they do here."

"I see, well we'll meet you at the pond," Swish said. "Enjoy your trip back. Hope you make it."

He and Fluff took off skittering along the limb when Randall called out.

"Wait, I didn't tell you…" he barked as he scampered after them.

Swish and Fluff stopped. "Tell us what?"

"When I reached the trees, I saw Watcher circling overhead, then glided toward the mountains. It felt as if he wanted to make sure we made it."

Who'd imagine an owl would care about three squirrels. This was a chittering chipmunk moment for Swish and Fluff.

"Thanks for sharing. Keep up, if you're coming," Swish said. *This owl is strange. They usually eat creatures like us.*

The two took off again with Randall following. As they approached the meadow, they saw their clan's home was nearer to the slimmest part.

"This'll be a quick crossing," Swish said to the other two squirrels. They scanned the sky, but didn't spot any shadows. They took a deep breath and ran.

Chapter 3

After seeing the squirrels make it safely into the forest by the pond, Watcher headed back to his old home. The lone owl surveyed the blackened sticks. The fire had wiped out everything. He searched again around the ruined stumps, hoping to find a sign his family had survived. But there wasn't any. He blinked from the sting of the smoke, which still clung to the remains of half-burned trees. Sadness swept over him like tumbling water over stones. With one last look, he departed to return to his new home.

Back at the pond, squeaks and cheeps from the kits and chicks joined in the springtime callings of creatures throughout the forest. The mornings were cool and the days warm. Short brief rain showers fell off and on, just as spring should be. Freddy, lounging on his lily pad, heard a little voice.

"Hi Freddy. We came to check out your pond."

Freddy glanced over and there were three little turtle heads poking up from the grass on the bank.

"Hi guys. Did it take you long to get here? How's JoJo and the family? Was there trouble with the fire?" Freddy asked.

"A day, they're fine and no trouble with the fire," James answered.

"Ha," croaked Freddy with laughter, "quick answers for me who has a mouth full of questions. I'm glad you came to visit the pond, hop in and I'll introduce you to the neighborhood," Freddy said.

They plopped into the water and followed Freddy toward the dam.

"See those holes in the dam?" Freddy pointed. "They let the river continue on its way. You need to stay away from them unless you want to take a trip downriver. Seymour didn't enjoy it at all, and I don't recommend it to anyone besides fish and beavers."

The three little turtles hissed with the terrible idea of fast-moving water.

"Let's stop and talk to Peanut while he's working."

During the fire, heavy rain had fallen and opened up a few extra holes in the dam. Peanut was examining his repairs to make sure they were holding up.

"Peanut, I want you to meet Peter, James and John, the turtles I told you about. They've come for a visit," Freddy explained.

"Nice to meet you and I hope you enjoy your time here. I'd stop and take a break if I could, but I need to finish inspecting the dam. It's a full-time job."

"We understand. Maybe later we can learn more on how you build them," James said. They left the dam and headed over to the lodge.

Toady had been spying from his log home when Freddy, with three other creatures, headed toward the beaver's home. *What? More nosey—whatever they are? I can't take it.* He left his log home and headed to his rock. He wanted to make sure these creatures knew he claimed this as his home.

While Honey harvested water lilies, the kits climbed all over the lodge. Freddy croaked a greeting as they swam toward the baby beavers.

When Bucky and Strawberry, the baby beavers, saw the turtles, they climbed off the roof of the lodge, and splashed into the water.

"Do you want to play chase?" Bucky asked. "That's a game Freddy and Seymour taught us."

James looked at his friends, and they nodded their heads. "Sure, sounds fun. Freddy, are you playing too?"

"I'm always ready for fun. I wonder where Seymour is? He won't be happy he's missing out."

16

After explaining the rules, Freddy told them he'd be it. The little beavers and turtles took off in every direction. Diving under, Freddy swam quickly toward one of the kits. With a tap, Freddy tagged Strawberry, and the game was on.

After a few rounds Freddy said, "That was fun and we'll play again sometime, for now there are more neighbors to meet."

The baby beaver's sad squeaks broke Freddy's heart as he ended the game. They didn't want the turtles to leave.

"It seems they love the turtles," Honey chuffed a laugh, "no I should say they love everybody."

Freddy spied Seymour sitting under Makula's tree, so Peter, James, and John followed Freddy to the little pond. Laying on top of his rock, Toady noted Freddy and the three trespassers as they climbed out and crawled toward Seymour. *Ah, they're nasty little turtles. I know how to handle them.* The chirps from the nest above drew Toady's attention.

"Hey, Seymour, what's going on?" Freddy asked.

"Just watch and you'll see."

With her beak, Makula pushed one chick toward the edge of the nest.

Freddy croaked in a panic, "Makula, what are you doing?"

She stopped nudging the baby and replied, "What every good parent does. I'm teaching them to fly."

"How is that teaching them? You're just pushing them out. Can't they learn to do it another way?"

"They were born with the knowledge of flying. What we teach them is how to use their wings. If they can't figure it out and they

17

get too near to the ground, Romero will scoop them up. Then they'll try again. Encouragement is what they need."

"If you say so." Freddy scrunched up his face. "Do you realize you haven't told us their names?"

Makula trilled with laughter. "Let me introduce them. This one here I should've called stubborn, in spite of that, his name is Bruno. He was the first to hatch." With that said, Makula gave a little push and off he went. He flapped and twirled, quick to get the hang of it. He touched down next to Seymour.

"This next one is Mateo, the typical middle chick. He was the second to hatch." She then pushed him out and off he sailed as if he had done it before. He landed on the other side of Seymour.

"This last one is Marina. She is sometimes shy and the smallest. I can't understand how I could've had such a timid chick." Makula nudged and pushed her on to the edge of the nest. Marina's grip tightened on a twig.

"You can do it, Marina," Freddy croaked.

Marina eyed Makula, then looked down over the edge again.

"You're stalling." Her mother said tapping her claw on the branch, "Your brothers flew with no problems and neither will you. Compared to your brothers, you're the littlest and lightest."

She shut her eyes and leaped off. Marina floated like a feather. She drifted and shifted from one wing to the other. She opened her eyes and with gentle gracefulness landed next to Freddy.

"Thank you, Uncle Freddy, for telling me I could do it."

Freddy's tongue did a fast flick, "Uncle?"

Makula joined her chicks and trilled with laughter, "Yes,

Freddy. I told my chicks you and Seymour were their uncles. We're family, right?"

"Yes, we are," Freddy grinned as he glanced over at Seymour, then saw the turtles standing behind him.

"Oh, I completely forgot you three were here. I didn't mean to ignore you."

He introduced them to Makula and her chicks. The young birds hopped around the turtles, peering down at them with one eye, then the other.

Little Marina asked, "May I touch your back?"

James answered, "Go ahead, you can't hurt us." Marina gently tapped James' shell with her beak. James clucked with his tongue.

Springing back, she asked, "Did I hurt you?"

"No, it tickled," James said, ducking his head into his shell.

Still sitting up in the nest, Romero saw Toady heading toward his chicks. He swooped off the limb and settled next to Makula.

Toady saw Romero join them, yet it didn't stop him from crawling up to the group to complain.

"Why are you three grubbers out of your tree?" Flicking his tongue toward the chicks. "You need to shut your chirping. I've had enough of this racket, and why are these other trespassers here?" He asked, glaring at the turtles.

James, Peter and John stared at the rude toad. They knew all about toads and avoided them as much as they could.

Makula hopped a little closer to Toady. "You need to mind your own business. My chicks were born here at the pond and have every right to go about as they please. Were you?"

Toady didn't say a word.

"No?" Makula asked as she leaned in, giving him the eye. "Well, I've had enough of your ill-mannered ways. You should just head back to your rock and stay there."

"I'll go where ever I want. I've claimed this area and I rule over it. I'm the toad master."

Makula trilled with laughter, "Where did you come up with that crazy notion? You have no power over anything."

Freddy had never seen Toady's face alter into such a dark green.

"Chrip-it." *You just wait nosey bird—you just wait.*

Marina watched Toady creep back to his rock. To her he looked sad and friendless. She felt bad for him. *Maybe I can make him happy.* She just had to figure out how.

Chapter 4

Anger churned inside Toady as he crawled back to his rock. *Who do they think they are, always dismissing me as if I was an ant crawling on the ground?* I eat ants. All the dumb creatures around his territory annoyed him and how they treated him.

"I'll show them," he grumbled as he climbed on top of his home. He glared at the group gathered by the little pond. The more he considered past comments, the angrier he became. He wanted to deafen them with his croak and stomp his feet. He wanted to make them wish they had never disrespected him that way. Up to now, the plans were slow to form.

"Sorry about Toady, we try to ignore him, but even with that, he continues to stick his tongue into everything around here," Freddy explained, smiling at the turtles.

"We've met a few nasty toads on our journey," James said. You better hope he grows tired of living here because when they get mad, they're mean."

"Yeah, we've heard stories too, and we're keeping an eye on him. It would make it easier if he would just move away. Except I don't believe it will happen. He's very stubborn," Freddy replied as he watched Toady climb on his rock. His attention returned to Makula when she spoke to her young.

"Come on back, you three. We need to keep practicing your take offs from the nest." Freddy watched as the three chicks lifted off and flew back to the branch.

He suddenly realized; how beautiful their feathers were when they flew. Freddy croaked, "Makula, when the chicks were born, they had dull colored feathers. Now look at them. Their feathers are similar in colors or a mix between yours and Romero. Why the change?"

"They're born with baby feathers, which are soft and warm and yes, very dull, but when they're older, the colorful ones replace the dull ones. It's a clue they're ready to fly."

"They did great for their first time. It took Seymour and me weeks to learn how to swim when our bodies changed."

Freddy directed his attention back to the turtles. "I'd like you to meet Ziggy and the crew. They're squirrels who live in the trees over there," pointing to one's close to Makula's. "But it might take forever for you to reach them."

"Hey, I'll hop over and give a yell," Seymour volunteered. With giant leaps, he headed over to Ziggy's home.

While waiting for Seymour to come back, Freddy and the turtles slid into the little pond.

James bobbed around in a circle. "This is very nice. Even though JoJo's pond is big, we don't have a special place to call our own."

Freddy showed the turtles the cave he and Seymour had used for safety. Freddy couldn't remember it being so small compared to the cave they spent the winter in. When they came out, they saw Seymour hopping back.

With a gigantic leap, Seymour jumped into the pond, splashing everyone. The wave pushed the little turtles, spinning them around. They laughed, but Freddy gave Seymour the look.

"What? That's a lot of hopping over to Ziggy's place and back. Anyway, Ziggy and the crew will be here soon."

Four squirrels dashed around a tree nearby. They leaped to the ground and raced over to the pond. The turtles along with Freddy and Seymour climbed out of the pond.

Before Freddy could introduce them, Ziggy spoke up. "I'm Ziggy and this here is Swish, Fluff and Randall. We're glad to meet you."

"My name's James, he's Peter, and that's John. They are simple names whereas yours are interesting."

Ziggy chittered a laugh, "Yes, we took nicknames which described our characters, including Randall. He's a snob."

Randall sputtered, "I'm not a snob, I'm—shall we say, well groomed?"

They laughed because he did sound snobbish.

Ziggy asked, "What brought you here to these parts?"

"When Freddy and Seymour were visiting JoJo, they said to come anytime, so here we are. We wanted to meet everyone and already we've played a few games with the kits and watched the three chicks fly for the first time. We've done more today than any other time since winter."

Ziggy looked toward Toady's rock. "Have you met him?"

"Yes, he's an unhappy creature."

"That's saying it nicely. Wish we could chat longer but we need to dash off, we have things to do. It's good to meet you. Hope to see you again," Ziggy chittered. The crew whirled around, zipped up the nearest tree, and quickly disappeared.

"Everybody moves so fast around here," James said in awe. Freddy croaked, laughing at the joke.

"One thing for sure, when it grows dark JoJo can hop fast," Freddy laughed again.

"Yes, I've seen him do that. Most of the time JoJo and his family enjoy relaxing and talking a lot. Sometimes he tells stories about the mountains where they came from."

This got Freddy's attention. He had heard none of these stories. *Maybe on the next visit I'll ask him.*

James asked, "Since it took us a while to reach here, would you mind if we stayed in your little pond for the night before we head back?"

24

"You're welcome to stay as long as you want," Freddy answered.

It was a splendid night with an abundance of stars twinkling in the sky, yet Watcher sat on his limb, sunk deep in sadness. Suddenly, a beautiful sound rose near Makula's tree. The owl perked up and scanned the area. Although he had superior night vision, what was making the melodious tunes stayed a mystery. He sat back on the branch, closed his eyes, and listened. He felt a deep peace come upon him.

Under his rock, Toady opened his eyes as the noise drifted through the air. He wanted to be mad, but it seemed to soothe him instead, which made him angrier. He didn't want to feel good.

Freddy heard it too. It was the same as when he was at JoJo's, except now it was nearby. He slid into the water and followed the sound. He wanted to find out what it was. He came upon the three little turtles staring up into the night sky and singing. He stopped and listened until they finished. *Their singing is strange, it gives me—peace—that's what it is.* He slowly swam back to his lily pad. *I should've woken Seymour. He'll be mad he missed them.*

Even though the song had been pleasing, he didn't understand the words. Something about...

'Who made the stars shine...'

Chapter 5

The next day Freddy swam to the little pond. The turtles were out of the water, lying near the edge. Their heads stuck out of their shells, while they tucked their legs up inside.

Freddy croaked as he swam through the cattails, "Good morning. How was your rest last night?"

"Oh, it was very nice. This is a cozy, peaceful pond," James answered.

Freddy made a quick leap and landed on the bank next to the three turtles. "I overheard you last night and your song was beautiful."

Embarrassed, John and Peter ducked their heads into their shells. Only their noses stuck out.

Their reactions surprised Freddy. "Why did they do that?"

James glanced at his friends and saw they wouldn't be much help as they ducked even further into their shells.

James stood up and shifted nearer to Freddy. He lowered himself until his shell rested on the ground. "They're just shy. They don't like anyone to notice them."

"I understand. Seymour was like that when we first met. So, tell me where did you learn to sing?"

"There was a gathering house next to the pond where we lived. The humans would sing all evening. Over time, we picked up a few words. We loved the sound, so we started singing."

"The first time Seymour and I heard you was when we were visiting JoJo. Why didn't they know it was you?"

James halfway ducked his head into his shell, "We don't want to trouble anyone."

"Trouble, you mean upsetting others?" It stunned Freddy. "Trust me, it wouldn't bother anyone. Well, maybe Toady." Freddy croaked a laugh as he glanced over to the flat rock. "He doesn't want to be happy, but I like how it made me feel. I say, sing whenever you wish."

"Thank you for telling us. We enjoy it, too."

That same morning, the owl flew over to Makula's tree. Perched next to her nest, she watched as he landed on the end of the limb.

"Good morning, Makula. May I ask if you caught the beautiful melodious tune last night?"

Makula was used to interacting with the enormous bird, however the chicks' eyes grew as big as beetle bugs at the sight of him.

"Yes, I did. Wasn't it splendid?"

"Do you know what made the music?"

"It came from below my tree. Unlike you, we don't see well after dark, and I couldn't tell."

As Watcher glanced down, he saw three little heads pop up out of the pond. They climbed out of the water and slowly walked toward Ziggy's tree. These creatures with their funny little bodies were new to the owl. Their backs appeared hard and shaped like a round rock. Their arms and legs stuck out in all directions.

"Look at who was in the pond," the owl hooted, gazing back at the ground.

Makula peered over the edge of the limb and saw the turtles. "Oh, it's Peter, James and John. Do you suppose it was them?"

"I do not know."

Near Ziggy's tree, something was tossing dirt into the air. A puff of dust hung over the area, resembling a cloud.

"Peter, John, let's check out what's going on," James said. They crept toward the fountain of dirt, and when they reached the source, they looked over the rim and saw Peanut digging in a ditch.

"Hi Peanut," James said. The beaver stopped and searched in the voice's direction. There sat the little turtles gazing down at him.

"What are you doing?" James asked.

Peanut chuffed a laugh. *Everybody loves to ask questions.* "Beavers are safer in water. I'm constructing passageways from the pond to the trees where we harvest our food. It seems safe around here, but we've had a few problems with wolves and foxes."

"But there isn't any water, though."

"Once I reach the trees up ahead, I will return to the pond and dig a small opening, then the water will seep into the canal."

"That's interesting and a good idea for turtles too. Would you mind if we use them once you're finished?"

"Not at all. I'm sure it will help you move around faster too," Peanut chuffed.

"Yes, that's true. We swim faster than we walk, which is tiring. Thanks for explaining." Peanut watched the three little heads disappear from the bank and went back to digging. *They sure are nice fellas.*

James and his friends headed back toward the little pond. As they passed underneath Ziggy's tree, James stopped and Peter bumped into him.

"Why did you stop?"

"I thought I sensed movement in the bushes," James whispered. They peered in and two gold beady eyes stared back at them. "Hide!" James yelled, and the three of them shoved their bodies into their shells.

Ziggy heard the yell and poked his head out. The same fox who bothered them in winter pounced on James. Ziggy chittered a call to the rest of the crew. They came skittering to Ziggy's tree. Once they saw what was happening, they grabbed pinecones and threw them.

"Throw nuts, they're harder!" Ziggy barked. The squirrels plucked the young nuts from the branches pelted the fox.

A good whack from Ziggy's nut caused the fox to drop James. It whipped around, leapt on the tree, and yipped at the squirrels. Dropping back to the ground, the fox picked up Peter with his teeth. A sharp crack rang through the air as he tightened his grip. Peter was in trouble and James shuddered. He waited for the next crack, when a loud screech and a rush of wind spun his shell around.

The owl swooped and raked his claws on the fox's back. The fox dropped the turtle and yelped. He whirled around to find out what caused such pain. Shivers traveled down his spine as an enormous owl descended upon him once again. His eyes widened with fear. Jumping into the bushes, he fled, leaving the little turtles shaken.

Still afraid, they stayed tucked up in their shells.

Ziggy chittered, "It's okay, the fox took off so you can come out now."

James stuck his head out, saw the owl gazing at him, and ducked back in.

"You are safe," the owl softly hooted. "I will not eat you. I prefer mice, although a nice juicy fox might not be bad for a change."

James stuck his head out, then his arms and legs. It took a little more encouragement to compel the other two out of their shells. James circled around Peter, inspecting his shell for any signs of damage, and was thankful not to find any. "How are you feeling?"

"I'm okay," Peter whispered.

After checking out each other's shells, they stared up at the owl.

To James and Johns surprise Peter spoke. "Thank you for saving us." These were the first words he had ever expressed to a stranger.

"It was my pleasure," the owl answered with a nod.

James asked, "Do you live around here?"

"I have been coming by this pond for some time, but I have recently made it my home." The owl decided not to inform the three he had seen them before.

The ruckus from the squirrel crew and the screech from Watcher had Freddy leaping toward the turtles. "James, guys, are you, all right?"

"Yes, thanks to the owl here. I think we should head back to our home. It isn't any safer here than there, and at least we know where Mr. 'gator lives."

Toady heard the screeching and came out from under his rock. Stretched out on top, he stared toward the squirrel's trees. *What now? These dumb creatures are always chittering or chirping about everything.*

Freddy was escorting the turtles toward the big pond, when Seymour arrived and asked what had happened.

"We just had a scare from a fox." James' shell shook with a shiver. "We're heading home."

From his rock, Toady croaked. "You should've listened to me when I told you to leave. Too bad the fox didn't take one of you with him."

Freddy's mouth dropped open in shock. "That's a terrible thing to say!"

"I'm just stating a fact. They should've left when I told them to."

"Ignore him, Freddy," Seymour urged, grabbing Freddy's arm.

"He's not just grumpy anymore. He's turning mean," Freddy fumed.

"Freddy, don't worry about him, he can't help it. He's sad and has no friends," James advised.

"I'm not sad, I'm unhappy! There's a difference. I prefer being alone, that's scarce these days. All these creatures won't shut their chirping, chittering and screeching mouths."

"Come on, Freddy, leave him be," Seymour said, tugging Freddy's arm again. The two frogs swam with the turtles to the other bank and waved goodbye.

"Remember to sing all you want. It makes everybody happy. Well, except for that one," Freddy said, pointing over his shoulder at Toady.

The owl heard Freddy encouraging the turtles to sing, so decided to guard over them as they journeyed home. He wanted to protect the special little creatures who had helped him find peace.

Chapter 6

Watcher remembered the first time he visited the Old Forest. Before he had left to seek his adventures, his father had given him wise advice. He had said, *'your life will serve a purpose when you search for opportunities to help others.'* Since then, he had followed his father's guidance and life had been rewarding.

He had plenty of time to sit and recall his first impression of this forest, as the turtles plodded below him. The trees were old, towering hundreds of feet high, and many had died long ago. The deeper the owl flew into the heart of the forest, the grayer the light grew, for the branches had interwoven together, making a braided vine canopy that blocked out much of the sunlight.

Where the dead trees had fallen over, openings in the canopy allowed pockets of light to filter through to the ground. In these pockets, bushes and slender trees flourished with intense green leaves. Drawn to the bright green, his eyes searched the dingy gray background for the next patch of light.

A smooth flight was almost impossible because of the moss hanging from the branches. When he first caught his wing in a tangle of moss, he plucked and pulled, using his beak, until he freed himself. He had learned to skim under the lowest branches, avoiding the moss as much as possible.

The little turtles arrived at JoJo's pond and slipped into the water. James turned to look up into the tree above him and spoke up. "Thank you for watching over us as we came through the forest."

Watcher opened his eyes wide in surprise, and just as quick lowered his lids halfway because of the light. "It was my pleasure."

Once they swam away from the edge of the pond, the owl lifted off to inspect the alligator. Because of the frequent rain showers, this swampy pond had expanded. He wanted to inspect his pool to see if it had done the same thing.

The owl landed in a tree where he had first seen the alligator. He scanned the banks. Not seeing him, he searched the water. The eyes were barely visible while the rest of his body lay below the surface.

Something disturbing caught his eye. A water path seeped toward where the turtles lived. *This is not good.* If the water continued in that direction, the alligator could follow it and find them. Watcher was wise about many things, yet he had no knowledge or ability to solve this problem.

He flew back to the turtles to inquire about speaking with the bullfrog. *How am I to talk without frightening him?* When he arrived, he saw a turtle on the bank. The owl landed a few steps away so as not to scare him. He wasn't sure which of the turtles he faced.

"I wonder if you would be kind enough to introduce me to the bullfrog family."

The little turtle peeked up at him, then slipped back into the water. *Strange,* thought the owl, then up popped another head, and this one climbed out of the water.

"Hi, John told me you want to meet JoJo?"

"Yes, I would. Why did John not speak to me?"

"John and Peter are both shy."

"You look very much alike," the owl confessed. "How can I tell you apart?"

"By our shells. There's what resembles a snake that goes from this leg," lifting his front left foot, "to my back leg," shaking his back right leg. "John has what's like bird wings and Peter has spots all over."

"Thank you for explaining your markings to me. Yes, would you introduce me to—JoJo?"

"Sure, I'll fetch him if you will wait here."

The little turtle slipped back into the pond and swam over to a pile of sticks that the owl guessed was the bullfrog's home. Not long afterward, a big bullfrog surfaced and swam over to the bank.

He leaped out and said, "I heard from the little guy that ya saved Peter from a fox. That was right, kind of ya. My name's JoJo. What can I do for ya?"

He speaks strangely. "Hello, I am Watcher. I needed to speak with you about a serious situation." He explained what he had observed at the alligator pond.

He be a right smart bird, JoJo thought as he squinted up at him. "This ain't good news. I don't rightly know what ta do. I need ta speak with Blossom, she be smart 'bout such things. Thank ya kindly for your concerns." He jumped into the pond and swam back home.

The owl waited for a few moments, not seeing him reappear, he left to hunt. *I will find out soon enough if they come up with a solution.* After catching a few mice, he returned and waited. When the owl observed JoJo swimming toward the bank, he descended from his perch.

"Blossom was thinkin' the beavers might know what ta do, so I'm headin' in that direction. I'd like your company, as you be the one who's seen what's happenin'."

"Yes, I will travel with you." The strange team left the swamp.

Watcher and JoJo reached the edge of Freddy's pond. *Much is happening here,* thought the owl. *It seems to be busier than usual.* The two sat and watched as the baby beavers played tag with Freddy and Seymour. The young chicks joined in the game, swooping, squawking and dipping toward the water. He didn't detect Toady. *Most likely hiding under his rock.*

JoJo took a deep breath, "Riibitt."

In an instant, all activity stopped. The entire group turned toward the bank and exploded in movement toward JoJo and the owl. The chicks flew down to perch on Bucky and Strawberry, bobbing their heads, trying to catch a glimpse of Billy Bob and Joleen to see if they were with their pa.

"Hi," Freddy croaked. "It's good to see you again. Where's the family? We were playing tag; can the kids play?"

"The family ain't here. We is here ta ask for help from the beavers," JoJo replied. The beavers, who were working on the dam, heard JoJo and swam to the bank. Makula and Romero noticed the gathering, and flew to land next to the owl.

Peanut's forehead crinkled with a puzzled look. "What's the problem?"

"Well, I best let Watcher here answer that, as he seen what be happenin'."

This must be serious, Peanut thought as the group gave the owl their full attention.

"After the turtles made it safely back to their pond, I flew over to view the alligator."

The group crowded closer together at the mention of the dreaded 'gator.

"I noticed that because of the rains, his pool has grown deeper. I also noticed a water trail seeping toward JoJo's pond, which could allow the alligator entrance to it."

Honey grabbed her kits, and the chicks fluttered into the air. She held them tight, moving closer to her mate, while squeezing the two frogs between her and Peanut.

"We must stop this somehow. With that being said, I do not have an answer on how to accomplish it," The owl confessed.

Freddy and Seymour popped out from between the beavers.

"Peanut, any ideas?" Freddy asked.

All eyes were upon Peanut. He sat there for a minute, thinking. He addressed Honey, "What about a dam between the two ponds would that help?"

Honey's worry-filled eyes rested upon Peanut as she answered, "It's impossible to decide on what to do until you view the situation and I can't leave the kits right now."

Freddy saw and understood Honey's concern for Peanut's safety. "He won't be alone; Seymour and I will go with him. Watcher and JoJo will be there too. He'll be safe."

"Okay, then I guess we're heading to JoJo's pond," Peanut said.

Chapter 7

This was the first time Peanut had been in the Old Forest. He noticed the trees differed from the ones he had used to build his dam. He smelled Ashe, Cottonwood, and Beech. They were splendid trees, although they smelled old. Many had died and fallen over.

The dead ones just might work. Peanut's mind was already working out a plan for a dam.

When Peanut, Freddy and Seymour along with Watcher arrived at JoJo's pond, the big bullfrog let out a *'WhooWee'* to let Blossom know he was home. Not expecting the loud call, Peanut jumped. Use to JoJo's bellow, the two frogs didn't even twitch.

JoJo gave Peanut an embarrassed look and croaked, "I'm mighty sorry 'bout that. Blossom don't like surprises."

"Oh, no problem, neither does Honey. First thing I need to do is survey the area. Is there anything dangerous I need to watch out for?" Peanut asked.

"Not 'round here, just don't be movin' in that direction," JoJo pointed over his shoulder. "That be where the 'gator lives."

They split up. The owl flew up to a tree and kept an eye on Peanut, while Seymour, Freddy, and JoJo swam over to Blossom and the kids to say hello. Then they returned to the bank to watch over Peanut.

Peanut waddled around the edge of the pond and then summoned them together.

"I need to put my eyes on the seeping waterway now," Peanut explained.

Seymour and Freddy shuddered, but they had to stay with Peanut.

"I will fly to where the alligator is while JoJo leads you on a safe trail," Watcher said. "I will wait there for you."

The owl left while Seymour, Freddy, and Peanut followed JoJo. Soon they reached the waiting owl.

"He is in his pool, and not on the bank. It is safe to view the waterway," the owl said, pushing aside a leafy plant. "Slip through here and that is where you will find the overgrown path which the

40

water is using to reach JoJo's pond."

They found the path and Peanut started walking toward the 'gators pond.

"Don't you be gettin' too close now," JoJo whispered a caution.

Peanut heeded the warning and didn't proceed further. After inspecting the path, he returned to the others, and waved for the owl to come talk with him.

"From this angle, I can't figure out which direction the water's moving toward. Is it following this path or spreading out?" Peanut asked.

"I do not know. I will scan the area."

They watched as the owl from a branch above peered one way, then the other. He flew over to another tree further away from the pool and did the same thing. At last, he came back and landed where the group waited.

Picking up a stick with his beak, Watcher drew a map of the pool and then a line showing the path the water crept along. He dropped the stick and said, "Here is where it starts." He pointed his wing to the pool. "It seems to follow the path we are standing on. There are no fallen logs which might prevent it from heading this way."

"Ok, that's good," Peanut remarked. "Did you notice how far it's traveled?"

"From what I observed, it has shifted a little toward JoJo's pond. Even with this, it is hard to draw any conclusions on where it would end up."

"That's okay. I've a plan," replied Peanut. "If I build a dam wall here on this end," pointing at the drawing, "and dig a channel running off this way," picking up the stick, he drew a line parallel to JoJo's pond, "I might stop it from progressing further. It won't be the same as our dam at home, still it will help change the course of the water. I might even loop the channel around to head back toward the alligator's pool."

"Oh, that be a mighty good plan there, Mr. Peanut!" JoJo said with an enormous sigh of relief. "My home'll be safe and Blossom's just gonna love it too. She'd be real pleased ta pull a trick on that beast. All he be is trouble."

Several small logs blocked the direction Peanut wanted to dig. He used them to build the wall and cleared the way for the canal. This way the 'gator would find no cause to leave the trail Peanut was preparing for him.

The owl did what he did best; he watched. He kept one eye on the alligator's location while observing Peanut at work. He had never met a beaver before. Peanut impressed and amazed Watcher by his hard word in building the wall.

Peanut was pleased and challenged to use his skills differently. Besides that, he enjoyed helping friends.

I could not find a better place to settle down than with this community of friends, the owl thought. *They are caring and hardworking.*

After the second day, Peanut consulted with JoJo and the owl. "I'm finished with the dam, now I can start this section of the canal which is the furthest from the 'gators pool. That way I can control the direction of the water," Peanut explained. "Watcher, could you keep me heading in the right direction?"

"Yes, I am assuming you want to curve back toward the alligator's pool."

"That's the idea."

He started digging, and the others followed behind him. The owl flew from one branch to another. This part went faster because he kept it shallow and the dirt was soft. The owl hooted a direction to Peanut, and he adjusted his course.

From time to time the bullfrog kids would come to the worksite and watch, then return to the pond to inform their ma and the turtles of the progress.

It seemed as if Peanut would burrow all the way to the mountains until the owl hooted to direct him to turn right and head back. After watching Peanut dig a few yards, Watcher left his perch to land next to the beaver.

"I believe you are close enough. The water will continue this course, correct? What is the next step?" The owl asked.

"Yes, I think the force of the water will continue this way. I'll return to the wall site now and dig toward the alligator's pool. Once I reach where the waterway begins, I'll connect my path with that one. It won't be enough to swim in, so I hope he prefers deeper water and never comes this way."

"Peanut—you are a wise beaver and a good friend."

"Thank you, Watcher, I couldn't have undertaken this task alone. If it hadn't been for you alerting JoJo to the problem, well, we won't think about what could've happened. I appreciate how you've taken care of for our little…" Peanut chuffed with a laugh,

"… or should I say our big neighborhood, as it appears to be growing every day."

Peanut got back to work and finished quicker than he expected. Amazed at his progress, the group stood back and viewed the success as water slowly trickled in. It gave the concept of a natural path.

Pleased with the results, Peanut grinned, "That should do it, though it wouldn't hurt to keep him under observation. I'm ready to return home. Believe it or not, I miss my kits."

Freddy and Seymour croaked with laughter, remembering how Peanut enjoyed the peacefulness of working on the dam.

"I will fly by once in a while. It is easier to view the results from a high up."

JoJo leaped high down the path with relief that Peanut had fixed the problem. *Yep, my Blossom's a right smart bullfrog. She know'd all along who'd help, but I bet she didn't know'd about the owl watchin' over us.*

The group split up when they reached JoJo's pond. Peanut couldn't wait to explain to Honey how great it turned out. It felt good to help the bullfrog family. Tuckered out from watching someone else dig and build dams, Freddy and Seymour were ready to lie around on their lily pads. It had been hard work.

The owl decided to stay awhile in the Old Forest. As night descended, he waited for the little turtles to make their way to the bank. Watcher closed his eyes as they lifted their heads to view the stars through an opening in the leafy canopy and sang as they had each night.

> '… does sadness fill my mind?
> As night becomes the day.

*A peace here I find when
from the heart we say ...'*

These were the perfect sounds of a peaceful forest home.

Chapter 8

Spring weather lingered, and life was good. There was plenty to do around the pond, so Freddy and Seymour didn't foresee any adventures for a while. Besides taking several trips over to JoJo's place, they played and shared stories with Tanks when he came by. On one visit, Tanks told them about a big fish who had taken up residence in his part of the river.

"I'm not sure where this fish came from. I'd say his school must have kicked him out. He's picked several fights with my friends and has injured a few of them. He understands I'm also a fighter, so he waits until I'm not around and then zips out to strike at them."

"What happened? Did he move away?" Seymour asked.

"Not right away. Together my friends and I made a plan where they surrounded me, and the fish wouldn't be aware I was in the center. When he came out, I struck first. I swam in and bit hard then dashed away. I charged at him several times until he gave up. I told him he better just head on down the river, because he wasn't welcome around here. I haven't seen him since, except I heard he picked on a young fish whose father was big and strong. Now he's gone for good."

Stunned, Seymour asked, "You mean the father killed him?"

"No, I mean a net picked him up. The humans got him," Tanks bubbled, swishing his tail. "I guess it's time for me to swim home."

"Don't stay away so long, we miss your visits," Freddy said. Tanks waved his fin goodbye and headed for home.

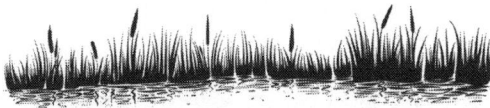

After fixing the problem with Mr. 'gator, JoJo and the family, along with the turtles, came for a visit. Because of traveling along the worn path between the two ponds, it was easy to follow.

Along with Billy Bob and Joleen, the group played above water games so Makula's chicks could be involved. The bugs were plentiful, to the delight of everyone, as at last the days warmed up. While feasting, Freddy and Seymour listened to JoJo's stories about his clan home.

"We got us a mighty big clan where we lived in Duck Bill Holler. Our pond be the largest in them there parts. Over in the next holler lived a feudin' clan. They was always fightin' with us. I don't recall why, howbeit my great grandpa Zeb said it'd been goin' on since he was a youngin'. Not a one of 'em knows the reason why. If I had ta guess, it be because of our pond. I think there was a fight over who owned it."

"That's why we decided to come here. We didn't want our youngins' gettin' their heads full of that nonsense. Anyways, one time my cousin Big T got caught in a trap set by a couple of humans. Along came a few of the feudin' clan. They surrounded him and poked him with sticks. A 'croakin' and a pokin'. Not a one helped him out. If it weren't for Big T's brother lookin' for him, the humans might a got to him first. I'm mighty glad we done left that place. We've got good neighbors, and that's what it's all about."

"We best be gettin' home, don't ya think?" Blossom asked.

The evening was upon them as JoJo examined the sky and saw the fading light. "Yup, it be time ta leave, give the youngin's a call. Thanks for your mighty fine hos-pe-tal-ity. Ya'll come a callin' anytime."

Even though the turtles loved Freddy and Seymour's little pond, they left with the bullfrogs. Disappointed with not hearing them sing that evening, the frogs waved goodbye from the other bank.

Toady was the only one happy about them leaving. He couldn't stand the singing and how it made him feel. He would scrunch deep under his rock and smash his hands over his ears every time they started that awful noise.

Not a day had gone by since the bullfrog family had visited with the neighbors when JoJo, leaving to check on the 'gator, whipped around after hearing a commotion. Was there a big animal thrashing around in the bushes? Instead, several pairs of glowing eyes stared back at him.

One huge bullfrog leaped out and croaked, "Well, if it ain't my cousin JoJo. We've been a lookin' for ya."

Then a large group of bullfrogs jumped out and, in a chorus sang, "We's come a callin'."

Blossom heard the voices and stuck her head out of the lodge. There were so many bullfrogs hopping all over the bank, she couldn't count them.

Joleen squeezed in next to her ma to take a peek. Her eyes grew enormous and then she glanced up at her ma, wondering what she thought. Her ma's face had changed into a deep spotty green. Joleen had seen that only once before. She backed away as fast as she could.

"What be all this here uproar?" Blossom bellowed.

The big bullfrog twisted around to face her, "Howdy, Blossom, we've come a callin'. It's been a long time since we seen our cousin. I hope it ain't a bother, us not lettin' ya know and all."

She was suspicious about why they were here. *Come a callin, huh? I ain't no fool. I'll be nice, except I be keepin' an eye on my treasures. Come ta think I best be hidin' 'em now.* She yelled out, "Nice ta see ya too, Bodean. Been awhile." With that said she stuck her head back in, gathered her treasures and left to hide them by an old rotten log.

JoJo, surrounded with them all talking at once, took a deep breath and croaked, "One at a time. Ya'll be worse than a bunch of chirpin' crickets."

Near to where the bullfrogs exploded from the bushes, the three little turtles cowered in their shells. They hadn't heard such a loud uproar in all their lives. With that many bullfrogs, it wasn't quiet anymore.

Once the turtles realized they weren't in any danger, they poked their heads out.

"What are we to do? They scare me," Peter hissed. John nodded.

James considered their options. "Maybe it's a good time to head back to Freddy and Seymour's."

The other two were quick to agree.

The owl sat on his perch above the pond and watched the uproar below. *What is this all about? It is not polite to overwhelm a family with visitors.* He hooted to himself as he observed the three little turtles creep out of the water further along the bank. *Yes, I would escape too if I could.*

JoJo was wondering the same thing. He hadn't been around his clan in a long time. He turned to Bodean, "Why did so many come ta my neck of the woods? It ain't normal. Ya always leave a few to watch over the place."

JoJo missed a glint of mischief in Bodean's eye as he poured out such a mournful woe. "It all be gone. Dry as a bone. No rain in a long while and home done dried up and blowed away. We come this way hopin' to find ya'll. Hopin' ta find us a new home."

JoJo felt bad for them, yet he also knew there wasn't room for the entire clan.

"Yer welcome ta rest a while, exceptin' this here pond ain't big enough for ya'll ta stay long."

JoJo glanced up at the owl. "Have ya seen any other ponds in this forest?"

"Not around here. Although, I have not been to the other side of the alligator's pool. I can search that way tomorrow and inspect the area. I need to check on him anyway," he hooted back.

Bodean hadn't noticed the owl. He slunk down, lying flat on the ground.

The enormous owl decided it was a good time to introduce himself. "I am Watcher. I protect this area and the areas beyond. I am a friend of JoJo's and his family, and I make sure no harm comes to them. If you hurt them, I will not be happy." *There, that will place a healthy fear in them and maybe we can avoid a disaster.*

Bodean nodded, "He be kin ta us, we're only lookin' for a new home."

The owl stretched out his wings and peered down at them, "That is good. I will search for a nice big pond."

That be a close one, I best be careful around him, Bodean thought.

Now JoJo was no fool. He'd make sure they didn't feel too much at home or they would push him and Blossom out of theirs.

Chapter 9

As Peter, James, and John marched along the well-worn path to Freddy's pond, they could hear the horrible clamor from the bullfrogs. *Do they call that singing? It's the worst noise I've ever heard,* James thought. The awful racket didn't decrease until they saw the last marker showing they were near the edge of the forest. *I'm glad we have some place to flee to. Poor JoJo and his family.*

"Not much further guys, I can see the clearing up ahead. Glad it's becoming quieter." The other two nodded as they followed James down the trail.

The turtles approached the bank of Freddy's pond, and everything appeared peaceful. Peanut was examining the dam, Honey was harvesting the water lilies, and the kits were soaking up a bit of sun on top of their lodge. Similar in peacefulness to what home used to be—until today.

Toady saw the three turtles on the bank of the pond. *Why are they back? They stay too long when they come and I can't stand their singing. It would please me big time to shut them up!*

The three slipped into the pond and swam over to where Freddy and Seymour were lounging on their lily pads. James stuck his head up next to Freddy. "Hi Freddy, we've come for another visit. Is it okay with you?"

Freddy sat up, "Sure, you can come anytime. The little pond needs visitors, and you three always keep it nice and tidy. How is everybody back at your pond?"

Before James could say a word, Peter piped up, "Way too much noise and way too many bullfrogs."

"What's this? Did JoJo have more kids? Freddy and I understand what it's like to have kids around," Seymour croaked a laugh.

Peter sunk under with just the tip of his nose showing. He had said enough.

James answered, "No, there's still just Billy Bob and Joleen, but JoJo's clan came to the pond. We didn't stick around long enough to hear their story; the noise drove us away. Watcher is there, he can explain what they said."

Freddy asked, "How many were there?"

"More than we could count."

"Wow, that's a lot of bullfrogs."

Hearing the voice of a turtle, Peanut swam over toward them. "Hi James, how are you? Come for another visit?"

"We're better now since we're away from the noise."

"What noise?"

"I'm surprised you couldn't hear them," James said. He again told of the clan visiting JoJo.

Peanut wasn't happy to hear that because too many bullfrogs can spoil a pond. He needed to speak with the owl right away. Peanut swung around and swam away.

"Did I say something wrong?" James asked.

"I don't know. He didn't appear to be happy to hear about the problem," Seymour said.

Peanut swam over to Makula's tree and hollered, "Makula, are you home? Can I speak with you?"

Toady heard Peanut and crawled to his spying place behind the tall grass. Makula stuck her head out, "Sure."

"Will you fly over to the Old Forest and ask Watcher to come here? I need to speak to him."

"I will go too," Romero offered. The two lifted off to find the owl.

What's that about? Toady wondered. He crawled to his log home. *If they meet on the other bank, I'll hear better.*

After the two birds left, Peanut went to find Honey and told her what James said. "I feel I should warn them. Watcher needs to

54

find out if there are any changes in the alligator's behavior."

When Makula and Romero reached the owl, they couldn't believe the noise. There were bullfrogs everywhere, dancing, diving and croaking in harsh sour notes.

"This is horrible," Makula said.

"What did you say?" Watcher asked.

Makula signaled for him to follow them.

Makula, Romero and the owl came out of the Old Forest and landed on the bank.

Peanut swam over, climbed out and got right to the point. "I'm concerned about the noise from all those bullfrogs."

The owl asked, "Could you hear them here?"

"No, James told us about the clan coming for a visit."

"Ah—yes, they are loud and I am glad to have a little peace, but I do not want to leave JoJo for too long. I sense dishonesty in this 'Bodean' who says he is a cousin."

"That's what I'm afraid of. The noise will bring the alligator to JoJo's pond like ringing a dinner bell to come and eat. Will you please check if the 'gator is becoming restless? If he is, it means he hears them and JoJo needs a warning." This upset Watcher. He left right away, heading toward the alligator's pool.

Toady flicked his tongue and clicked his lips together, laughing at their troubles.

Back at JoJo's pond, the clan was making themselves at home. The rising of the noise level had already driven the turtles from the pond. While the owl flew to observe the alligator, JoJo's clan sang a rowdy chorus.

'If I were a bullfrog,
this is what I'd do.
I'd sing a song so loud and strong,
there'd be nothin' you could do.'

JoJo, Blossom and the kids were in their little house covering the sides of their heads, trying to soften the clamor. *Oh,* thought Blossom, *Ain't they never gonna leave?*

The owl landed in a tree overlooking the 'gator's pool. *He has to be hearing the commotion.* He could hear it himself, and noise travels well in water. The alligator's tail whipped back and forth, slapping the water. He let out a roar. Waves formed in the pool as he rolled and thrashed about. Slowly he rose and climbed out. His snout pointed toward JoJo's pond. *I need to warn JoJo now before he figures out where the noise is coming from.*

Watcher flew back to JoJo's and screeched. JoJo slid out from under his house and poked his head up out of the water.

The owl hooted, "JoJo, come to the bank!" When JoJo hopped out, Blossom and the kids were right behind. The owl landed next to him, "You must quiet them. The alligator can hear the noise and it will draw him here."

Facing the rowdy bullfrogs, JoJo bellowed in alarm, "Keep it down or ya'll be eaten!" JoJo turned to his mate and kids, "Quick, take off for Freddy's pond. I'll try to quiet 'em."

Blossom spoke to the youngin's, "Ya'll go ahead, I'll be right behind ya, just got ta get my treasures."

"Ma, we can help. You cain't carry it all. If'n we split it up, we be a travelin' faster," Billy Bob croaked.

They headed to where Blossom had hidden her treasures. She divided it between the three of them, wrapped them in big leaves and left for the path to the big pond.

Bodean observed Blossom and the kids skedaddling along a path. *Hah! It be workin'. They be movin' out and we can take this here pond for our own.*

JoJo puffed up at Bodean, "I told ya'll ta get quiet."

Bodean said, "Look li'l cousin, we be celebratin' our stoppin' by. Don't ya miss singin' with us? Join in why don't ya."

JoJo said, "I need you ta get quiet like. There be a 'gator close ta here. Yer makin' too much noise and you be callin' him ta dinner."

"Ah JoJo, ya always could tell such big whoppers. Now go on, sing with us." Bodean twisted around and joined right back in. He gave JoJo a sideways glance as he watched him leap away from the bank.

Hah, thought Bodean, *This here pond be ours now!* "Come on, fellers let's take a dip." The entire clan leaped into the pond and started another rowdy chorus.

> *'Ain't nothin' better than takin' a dip.*
> *In a pond so fine, it clears the mind.*
> *Ain't no better way to say,*
> *but this here, pond we claim today.*
> *So, sing real loud and splash about*
> *for we is here to stay.'*

The alligator had found his way to the pond and hunkered down on the bank. The owl flew up to a perch right above him while JoJo hid under a large leaf. Watcher screeched a warning. All the bullfrogs glanced up at the owl, and then their eyes traveled to what lay beneath him. There sat a monster with wide-open jaws and sharp, jagged teeth. The 'gator surged into the water. The bullfrogs reacted fast, leaping out onto the other bank and into the brush surrounding the pond. The 'gator's jaws snapped toward Bodean; yet luck was on his side. He hopped out, but not before he felt the furious breath of death on his back.

Mr. 'gator swam around JoJo's pond as if he had found a new home. His tail whipped around and smashed in to the bullfrog's house. JoJo was heartbroken. Gone was all his hard work with a swipe of a tail.

Bodean came over to JoJo. "I'm right sorry I didn't listen to ya. I figured you was jestin' with me. Thanks for warnin' us. I truly be feelin' mighty bad 'bout your pond. I guess it ain't safe no more. Me and the clan had better git goin' as ta find us a new home."

"I'm good and mad at ya, still I'm mighty glad ya didn't get hurt. I'm gonna warn ya, there be a pond over yonder that ain't for you. That's where my family fled to because ya wouldn't listen. I'm a hopin' ya find someplace else real soon."

Chapter 10

It upset JoJo. After all of Peanut's hard work in keeping his pond safe, he lost his home and almost lost his family. The owl flew down and joined him.

"You tried to warn them; however, they did not listen. It is not your fault. You did not lure the alligator here, and you are not responsible for their actions. Come, let us join your family. They are probably worried about you."

Watcher and JoJo left for Freddy's pond. He stopped for a moment to turn back and saw Mr. 'gator swimming around the ruins of his old home. His hops didn't possess much of a spring as worried thoughts rolled through his mind. *What are we ta do? Where's my kids gonna grow up? Winter ain't long from now.* Then JoJo stumbled mid-leap with the thought, *Blossom's gonna be real mad.*

Meanwhile, the community had gathered around Blossom and the kids. The squirrel crew along with Makula, Romero and the chicks had joined them on the other bank. They waited and watched, hoping everything would be all right. At last, Watcher flew out from the forest. Blossom cried puddles and puddles of tears as she spied JoJo hopping toward the pond.

"I thought for sure you be a goner," she croaked, gulping big breaths to stop the tears. "I'm so happy ta see ya."

Embarrassed with all the commotion, JoJo's face faded to a pale green, "There, there, it ain't nothin' ta go on about. I'm here."

The entire community wanted to hear what had happened. JoJo was still too mad about it and didn't want to say something he'd regret later so, the owl explained.

"It was a close call, but nobody got hurt. JoJo tried to warn them, but they figured he was making up a story. Because of the noise, the alligator found their pond and scattered the bullfrog clan."

They gasped in horror of what could've happened to the bullfrogs. No one had considered the alligator to be an actual threat. Now they faced the ugly truth.

"Your clans not coming, here are they?" Peanut asked.

"Nope, I made it clear this here pond was not for them. They were right sorry ta have ruined our home."

"What are we gonna do, JoJo? We can't go back now." More tears slid down Blossom's face.

With a frantic jolt JoJo twirled around, his eyes focused on the Old Forest, "What about the turtles, I didn't see the turtles, quick we got ta save 'em."

"JoJo, they're all right," Freddy croaked. "They came here earlier and they're safe in our little pond."

"Oh, I'm so relieved. Don't think I coulda stood it if anythin' had happened to 'em. I don't know what me, Blossom, and the kids are gonna do now."

Freddy scanned the gathering, and they all nodded. "By a vote we took, you're welcome to live here. You've always been like family, so please make this your home. And the turtles are welcome too."

Toady had been lounging by his log home when he heard the announcement. "Now wait just a minute. I demand you listen to me," he bellowed.

Watcher gazed over at Toady, "Yes? Is there something you would like to say?"

Toady flicked his tongue, "You don't scare me, I'm a toad and I rule over this place. These creatures are not welcome here. It's too crowded and they must leave."

The owl noted his friends' displeasure toward Toady's announcement. "If I recall, we did not vote you as ruler. Shall we take a vote now? As a group, you have maintained and preformed a wonderful job in governing yourselves. What do you say?"

Makula screeched, "I vote no to Toady ruling over us." The rest raised their voices with an overwhelming vote of no.

"You heard the vote. Head back to your rock or you are free to leave the area."

"I will do as I please, no matter the vote. You will regret this, and you can count on me making you miserable, that's for sure. Chrip-it!" Toady shifted around and crawled back to his rock, instead of climbing on top he slid under it.

"Back to the primary point, we agree you are all welcome here," Watcher replied.

Blossom burst out crying again, and all the creatures laughed because they knew they were tears of happiness. When she could speak, she said, "Thanks ya'll for havin' kind hearts. We're so blessed ta have such good friends."

The kits, chicks, and kids exploded with croaks, chuffs, and chirps because now they could play together all the time, and off they went, churning the surrounding water.

The next day, while the kits and kids were playing a game of chase, Makula perched on the beaver's lodge with Honey to keep an eye on them. They were having a lengthy discussion on raising kits and chicks. "The old saying is little chicks have big ears," Makula said.

"Yes, you could say the same about kits," Honey agreed as she groomed and smoothed out her coat.

This talk confused Freddy, as he squatted on a lily pad listening. "What does that mean?" He asked as he studied one face then the other.

Makula ruffled and cleaned her flying feathers. "It means chicks hear everything we talk about."

Freddy shrugged, "Yes, I understand that, why is it bad?"

"There're things the chicks need not hear. They need to play, have fun, and not worry about the threatening stuff."

"And neither should the kits," Honey agreed.

Freddy still didn't understand what could be wrong with the little ones hearing about things which mattered, but he let it be. Saying goodbye to the two of them, he swam to search for Seymour.

Makula glanced toward her tree, but didn't observe anyone in the nest. "I better see what my chicks are up to. It's a little too quiet around here."

"I understand what you mean. Quiet is not a good sign," Honey replied. "My problem is, if they're playing underwater games, it isn't easy to find them until they surface. Well, I'm heading out to harvest a few more water lilies while I have the chance."

Makula lifted off the lodge and flew to Ziggy's tree.

"Ziggy, are you here?" Makula called out.

Ziggy stuck his head out. "Hi, can I help you?"

"Yes, I was wondering if you've spotted my chicks? I haven't seen them for a while."

"No, I haven't. I've been in the forest behind my home, gathering nuts."

"Thanks. I'm sure they're with Romero, at least I hope they are."

Meanwhile, Freddy found Seymour over by the little pond. When the turtles came to live there full time, they renamed it Turtle Pond.

"Hey what are you guys doing?" Freddy asked.

Toady slipped up to his grassy spying place to listen to their conversation.

"We've been talking about how they first came to live at JoJo's pond," Seymour replied.

Freddy plopped down beside Seymour. "I want to hear too."

James continued their story. "We aren't brothers, or at least we don't believe we are. Peter, John, and I met at the pond next to the 'gathering house' where little humans named us and we were happy to be together. When they came to visit, they fed us and played with us."

"Over time, though, they stopped coming. Food became scarce and our pond dried up. We had to find a new home; still it was hard to leave. We loved listening to the humans sing and we miss it."

"We wandered through a meadow and for a while we believed we were walking in circles because we had a limited view through the tall grass. Even with that, we finally reached a forest."

"We came across a small shallow pool. A tree leaned over the water and underneath it, the bank had worn away, leaving a tiny cave. The roots created a secure barrier from the rest of the pond. It was pleasant, so we stopped to rest. This is where we almost lost John."

Freddy and Seymour sat up, double flicked their tongues, and stared at John. John ducked his head into his shell as his legs trembled, remembering his brush with death.

James continued, "A creature crept up on us. Peter heard a noise, glanced over, and spied a black striped face. He hissed a warning, and we dove to the bottom. Quick as we could, we swam through the tangle of roots. The last to arrive was John."

"The creature took a swipe at him, which spun John around in a circle. His hard shell had saved him. He dove to the bottom and climbed up through the roots. We hid against the bank until the creature gave up trying to reach us. We're thankful that was the only scary part of our journey to a new home. And now you know how we came to JoJo's pond."

"What an adventure. I know what it's like to face a beast. I'm glad you live here now. We enjoy your singing, and Turtle Pond needed someone to take care of it," Freddy said.

Makula returned to her nest from Ziggy's. Noticing the gathering under her tree, she called out.

"Have any of you seen my chicks?"

"We saw Mateo and Marina fly off with Romero a little while ago," said James. "But we haven't seen Bruno."

Upset, Makula asked, "Which way did Romero head?"

Seymour pointed upstream, and she took off in that direction.

Freddy and Seymour were both a little worried. What popped into Freddy's mind was what Makula and Honey were talking about earlier, how little chicks had big ears. *What did Bruno hear and where did he go?*

While Makula was asking about her chicks, Toady crept out from his hiding place.

"Seems like trouble has settled on this place. It's all because of you," pointing at the turtles. "You seem to draw attacking beasts. All you produce is misfortune," Toady said.

James crawled up to him, "It's okay, Toady. Maybe we do, but Watcher is here, and he takes care of us."

"Don't you ever call me Toady again! Hear me?"

"Isn't that your name? That's what Freddy calls you. If it's not your name, what should I call you?"

"My name is none of your business, and that owl won't always be watching. Then you'll be in trouble." Toady had enough of dealing with this creature. With a flick of his tongue, he crawled away.

"Since we're neighbors, we'll be around, Toady. Maybe we could try to be friends."

Toady stopped, turned around, and crept toward James.

"I told you not to call me that, and I don't want to be your friend. I know all about turtles, and how to mess with them."

In horror, the others watched as with a quick flick of his tongue he wrapped it around James' leg, flipped him over, and then crawled toward his rock. He climbed on top and smacked his lips with pleasure as he glared at the others.

"Quick, flip him back over," Peter cried. Freddy and Seymour grabbed James' shell and righted him.

"What an evil thing to do," Freddy yelled at him.

"What are you going to do about it?" Toady croaked back.

Freddy took a deep breath. "Not a thing—Toady."

"It's about time you become afraid of me."

Before Toady could say another word, Freddy leaped over to him and spoke in a low voice. "I'm not afraid, I'm just better than you. If you ever attempt that again, I'll make sure you're banished from the pond."

"You can't. You don't have the power—"

"Maybe I do, or maybe I don't, but I don't think you'll want to find out." Freddy hopped back to the others.

Chapter 11

While Makula flew off to find Romero, Freddy and Seymour left Turtle Pond and swam to Peanut and Honey's lodge. When they arrived there, Bucky and Strawberry were swimming circles around Honey. "Please Maw, please can we go now?" the two begged.

"Did you get everything done?"

"Yes, but I don't think it's fair I had to help him," Strawberry said, thumping Bucky with her tail. "He's the one who brought that stuff in."

"Stop it," Bucky said as he thumped her back. "I like rocks."

"Still do you need to sleep with them?"

"I want to keep them safe."

"Who's going to take them? I don't enjoy sleeping on lumpy old rocks."

"You heard Maw talk about the thief. Maybe he's still around. He might try to steal them."

"Your rocks aren't special like Maws," Strawberry whined.

"Okay, stop it you two, I've heard enough and I don't imagine Freddy and Seymour want to hear it either. Right?"

Freddy opened his mouth, but Seymour jabbed him in the side.

"Why did you do that?" Freddy asked.

"Because it's between Honey and her kits."

Honey chuffed a laugh, "Go ahead, you can swim over to Billy Bob and Joleen's, though don't get in JoJo's way. He and Blossom are trying to build their home."

"We won't," Bucky said. "They want to call on the turtles."

"If the turtles are busy, you leave them alone too. Do you hear?"

"Yes, Maw, we hear you," the kits said in unison.

"Come on, Strawberry. Let's leave before she changes her mind." Bucky tugged on Strawberry's tail.

"Wait, before you go, have you seen Bruno?" Freddy asked.

"No, we've been inside cleaning our room," Strawberry said, plucking Bucky's fur. He then gave Strawberry's ear a tweak. Maw touched their heads, and they settled down.

Freddy flicked his tongue. "You clean your room? What's there to clean?"

"Trust me Freddy; they haul all kinds of stuff in," Honey replied. "There isn't any room to sleep."

Bucky ducked his head. "I like to gather rocks and twigs. Maybe I pick up too many."

"I enjoy collecting too," Honey said, "You need to just pick special ones."

"They're all special to me."

Honey noticed his disheartened look, and her heart gave a tug. "Maybe we can make a place to organize your rocks and such so Strawberry doesn't have to sleep on them."

Bucky perked up and joy lit his whiskered face, "That'd be great, Maw. Can we do it right after we play with Billy Bob and Joleen?"

"Sure, now take off," Honey chuffed. With a thump of their tails, the kits sped away.

Honey gave Freddy her attention. "What were you saying about Bruno?"

"Makula hasn't spotted him since their morning meal. She flew up stream to find Romero hoping Bruno had joined them."

"When Makula and I were talking earlier about big ears, I saw Bruno fly overhead. She must've not noticed him," Honey said.

"Did you see which way he went?"

"It appeared as if he was following the owl into the Old Forest."

Oh, I wish he hadn't gone in there, Freddy thought.

Seymour asked, "Do you think Watcher asked Bruno to go with him?"

"I doubt it, at least not without seeking Makula's permission first."

"I guess you're right," Seymour said. "He'd never cause Makula to worry. Look, here comes Makula and Romero. I only see two chicks. I guess Bruno didn't head that way."

Honey waved to get their attention, and the family of birds landed on the bank near the lodge.

"I'm sorry, Makula," Honey said. "I figured you saw Bruno fly overhead when we were talking this morning. He followed Watcher into the Old Forest."

Makula whipped around to stare at the forest. She screeched in panic, "Romero, he heard us talking about the alligator. Do you think he went to look for it?"

"Si, I'm most worried about him. He is stubborn. When we tell him no, he does anyway. We must search." He turned to his other two chicks. "You stay with uncles, we be back. You two, no go anywhere."

The chick's eyes were wide, and they nodded.

"We promise. Don't let the alligator eat him," Marina cried.

Romero covered them with his wing to soothe them, "Do not worry. We will find him."

Makula pecked her young birds on the head, and in a hushed

croon said, "I love you both. Please be good and listen to your uncles." Turning to Romero, she said, "We need to hurry. It's been a long time since anyone has seen him."

"Si, si, we leave now."

As she lifted away from the bank, she heard Honey call out.

"Find Watcher, he'll help you search."

Fear gripped Makula as a horrible thought continued to roll through her mind. *Don't let it be too late, don't let it...* Her wings took deeper strokes as they flew toward the Old Forest.

It felt as if it took forever to reach the trees, though it was just a few quick seconds. Makula screeched at Romero, "We've been to JoJo's old pond, should we start there?"

"Si, good place."

When they arrived, they surveyed the surrounding trees, checking for any signs of Bruno or the owl. The pond appeared to be safe, except they knew how sneaky the alligator could be so they didn't draw close to the water.

Romero screeched when they landed on a limb which hung over JoJo's old pond. "Watcher—are you here?" Silence greeted them. Again, though louder, "Watcher—are you here?"

Makula paced back and forth on the limb. "We need to find Bruno."

"Patience. First, we find the owl. We do not know where alligator lives."

"I understand, but our chick's alone in this horrible forest." Makula stopped pacing and slumped low onto the branch.

A whisper of wings announced the owl's appearance from

deeper in the forest. "I heard your call, what is wrong?"

"Our chick, Bruno, follow you here. Have you seen him?" Romero asked.

"No, I have not. Why would he come here?" Watcher asked.

"We think Bruno heard us talk about alligator. He might come look," Romero said.

"Please help us find him," Makula screeched, raising her wings.

"Yes, of course." *Will we find him in time, though?*

Chapter 12

As Makula and Romero were talking to the owl, Bruno was circling the alligator's pond. He couldn't see it as he searched the water. *Maybe I need to get closer.* He flew to a low-hanging branch right above the water.

The alligator noticed the colorful bird and glided under the water toward it. He rose bit by bit, keeping everything except his eyes below the water. He watched as the bird settled on a branch within his reach.

As Bruno leaned over and peered down, the alligator leaped out of the water. Startled, Bruno screeched. His wings whipped up as he sprang backwards. He felt the whoosh and heard the crack of snapping jaws. The alligator roared as he barely missed his target.

"Did you hear that?" The owl twisted his head around. "We must go NOW!"

More startled screeches and frantic cries followed. Romero burst through the trees to find Bruno caught in a web of moss and hanging close to the gapping mouth of the beast. Each time the alligator lunged at Bruno, he brought his wings in with a downward thrust to lift himself up and away from the jagged row of teeth. Bruno panicked as the last lift cleared him only inches from the beast's powerful jaws. He was tired and losing strength.

With a calm tone Romero said, "Bruno, we are here, do not be afraid."

Time was important, and they didn't waste any as the three discussed a plan to distract the alligator so Romero could help Bruno free his wings. A burning feeling flooded through Bruno's wings as he heaved away from the 'gators sharp snapping teeth.

Watcher hooted instructions as he circled the pond. "Bruno, your Mother and I will charge at the alligator to make him follow us."

He shook his head. "No, Mamá, don't come too close. He's fast."

"Do not worry, she is smart and understands how to stay away from his teeth. While we distract him, your Father will help free your wings. Listen to what he tells you. Understand?"

Bruno nodded. The owl and Makula dove, screeching at the alligator, taunting him to alter his course away from the young chick. The owl scrapped his claws across the top of the alligator's head and he lifted out of the water and charged him. The jaws snapped shut, catching air. The owl was faster.

Angry, the alligator lunged at them and they backed away. On went the death dance between them, leading him farther from the little chick. Romero reached his son. With his beak, he ripped at the moss holding the right wing.

"Pull, Bruno, pull wing down."

Even though it shifted a little, there were still strands holding the outer edge. Romero shredded those, pulling with all his might. Bruno's wing popped free. With one wing free, he could slide the other out from the tangle of moss.

Romero screeched. "He is free let us leave."

They flew away from the snapping alligator. He twisted around to return to its prey. As he approached, he let out an angry roar. His snack had escaped.

The four flew back to their pond. Bruno, tired and shaken from the narrow escape, felt bad for placing his mother and father in danger. *I will never go back there again.*

Mateo and Marina skaawed when they saw their brother safe.

"Thank you, Watcher. I cannot say what means to me," Romero said.

"I am glad I could help." He turned his attention to Bruno. "Young chick, you were fortunate this time. However, next time you might not be as lucky."

Bruno hung his head. "Yes, Watcher, I'm sorry to cause trouble.

I'll be good."

Makula glanced at the owl. "I was wondering—why do you return to the Old Forest? The turtles and bullfrogs are safe and living here."

"There are a few animals driven from their homes when the fire burned them out and I am watching over them. I am ready for a rest; I will see you tomorrow." The owl lifted off the bank and headed for his home on the other side of the squirrel trees.

Makula thought about what Watcher said for a moment. Then one of her chicks complained they were hungry. She rolled her eyes and Honey chuffed with laughter. Yes, whether it be chicks, kits or bullfrog kids, they were always hungry.

JoJo and Blossom settled in after finishing their stick home, which they had built just past the beaver's lodge. The big bullfrog was taking a nap on a water lily when he felt the water stir around him. JoJo opened one eye and watched as Peanut approached.

"Hi JoJo, I hope I'm not disturbing you. I wanted to study how you built your house. It appears to be like mine," Peanut said as he swam around the pile of sticks.

"I be mighty glad ta show you around," JoJo said as he slid into the water. He first took Peanut underneath.

Peanut came back up to the surface. "That's interesting how you use the lily pads as a base. I wouldn't guess they could hold the weight."

"Well ain't nothin' to it. I gather the pads so there's lots of 'em hooked together like, in one spot."

Peanut dove under to check it out again and popped back up. "That's a clever idea. Is this how you built homes where you lived with your clan?"

"Nope, it be my own design. My clan lived in caves. I don't rightly take ta livin' in the dark. Neither does Blossom. We wants ta get in and out of the water, quick like."

Peanut looked toward his lodge and observed the distance. "Why did you build your home in this part of the pond?"

"Well, way back, when I was jest a youngin', no older than Billy Bob, my pa used ta say, *'It ain't polite ta camp at your neighbors' front door'*. I figured this be far enough away from yer place."

"Close, yet not too close. What a perfect way to view it," Peanut laughed. "Your pa was very smart, and I'm happy we're neighbors. I better head back to the lodge and see if Honey needs anything, before I return to work." Peanut swam away, but JoJo's home was still on his mind.

As Peanut climbed up into the lodge, he asked Honey, "Have you seen how JoJo built their home? It's a resourceful use of lily pads. I wouldn't have thought it possible."

"No, I haven't, but I'm not surprised. They're friendly and practical, even if they talk strange. I figure they'll be a nice fit to our community and the kits enjoy playing with the youngin's, as Blossom calls them," Honey chuffed a laugh.

"Yep, I'm glad too. I guess I'll be heading back to work on those canals, unless you need me to do something. I've almost finished with this last one and I want to get some use out of them before winter."

"The kits and I are fine. We'll be harvesting water lilies for dinner."

Peanut had finished a few canals already and thought a few more would be nice. Keeping the kits safe in the water was a top priority. He was pleased to note the turtles and frogs were using them too.

Honey had been educating Bucky and Strawberry on what plants were safe and which ones were poisonous. Makula was doing the same with her chicks. On this particular morning, Freddy watched as Makula instructed them on safe berry picking.

"Look very close at these berries. Marina, are you paying attention?"

Marina had been watching the squirrels instead of listening. Turning back to the bush, she said, "Yes Mamá, I see them." She stretched out to peck one...

"Stop! These are poisonous. Your life depends on you heeding these lessons."

Marina's wings slumped, *I can't help it, I want to be playing, just the same I want to stay alive too.* Peeking up, she said, "Yes, Mamá."

"Very well. Now over here are the good berries. Look at the leaves—" a squeak from one of the squirrels made her swing her head around to catch sight of what had happened.

"Marina!" Makula glared at her chick.

Freddy and Seymour enjoyed watching the squirrels play too.

The squirrel crew had several games, same as the frogs, though theirs had nothing to do with water. One was who could glide the farthest from tree to tree. The other was tag. They flipped, bounced, and spiraled up and down the trunks. Sometimes they were just a blur of fluffy fur. They even made a game out of gathering food for the winter.

As Freddy was watching the squirrels, it reminded him of the games they played with their fish friend, Tanks. Neither he nor Seymour had seen him for quite some time and wondered how he was doing.

"Hey, Seymour, what do you think about visiting Tanks? Are you up for another adventure?"

"Sure, I've been wondering how he's doing."

Freddy and Seymour went to notify Peanut where they were going, except he wasn't at the dam. They swam toward the lodge to find Honey where she and the kits were harvesting lily pads. Well, Honey was harvesting, Strawberry and Bucky were snacking more than gathering.

"Hi Honey, keeping busy?" Freddy asked.

Honey looked at her little ones, "A few of us are working more than others." Bucky and Strawberry grinned as they munched on the water lilies. "Was there something you needed?"

"Yes, Seymour and I are leaving for Tanks' place."

"That sounds fun. Enjoy yourselves and thanks for telling me," Honey replied.

The community had a new rule. It had become clear some things needed to change when first Billy Bob, then Bruno, had gone missing. Since neither one had told their parents they were taking off, no one knew where to begin their search. The community decided if anyone was leaving the pond; they needed to notify someone who was staying.

There wasn't a cloud in the sky and a warm early summer breeze brushed over them as they hopped along the trail. This would be an effortless trip for the frogs, because they weren't dragging the hauler, they used to move Tank's nugget. Several times they had stopped to rest and cool off in the shade.

Once they found the fallen tree and slid under it, all they had to do was find Tanks hole in the ground. There were several holes, but after a bit of a search they came across the right one. There was Tanks treasure, shining as bright as ever.

Freddy sighed, "It's still the prettiest rock I've ever observed. Now let's find Tanks."

Chapter 13

Seymour looked concerned. "Uh, Freddy? How will Tanks know we're here?" he asked, gazing into the hole where the sparkling nugget lay in the water. Tanks had been lucky to find a natural cave which opened from the river. It was the perfect spot for him and his visitors to view the rock.

Freddy squinted at Seymour, trying to understand what he was talking about, when the problem became clear. He plopped himself down and croaked, "I didn't think of that."

They sat for a while trying to come up with an idea.

"Maybe we should head back home," Seymour suggested.

"What? I'm not heading home yet. Come on Seymour, you're smart, think."

Seymour hopped around in a circle. Freddy watched, though said nothing to interrupt Seymour's thought processes. He dropped beside Freddy. "First, we need to find water. My skin's dried out and when I'm uncomfortable, my brain doesn't work very well. Besides, we need it to talk to Tanks."

"There isn't any water between here and our pond, maybe we should continue further downriver."

"I don't know. What if there isn't any that way either?"

"Come on, just a little further, if we don't find any water we'll head home."

They found what appeared to be a path. It wasn't more than a line of dirt between the plants, yet it led in the direction they wanted to travel. Though there were fewer bushes to deal with, these weren't easy to squirm through.

Seymour stopped. "Freddy, I hear water."

"I've been hearing it too since we've been hopping next to the river."

Seymour gave Freddy the squinty-eyed look. "Really, you need to give me a small amount of credit. I hear a trickle of water, not just a river roar. Okay? We might find it on the other side of these bushes."

Freddy gave Seymour a flick of the tongue, "A little touchy, are we? Ever hear of a joke?"

"I told you I'm hot, dry and thirsty."

They crawled under a few thorny bushes, and there in front of them was a tiny stream trickling toward the river.

"Let's hop in, Seymour, and find where we end up."

The two frogs entered the shallow stream. After rolling over several times to wet their dry backs, they slipped over slimy stones and slid toward the river. In some places, it shrunk into a puddle where they had to climb over rocks to cross into deeper water. At last, they heard the rumble of rushing water.

Drawing closer, the stream widened and cascaded over the edge into a shallow inlet. Freddy and Seymour leaned over for a better view. Below the tiny waterfall, the water lapped gently against the dirt wall. The river had slowly eroded away the bank, and the water was calm so it wouldn't push them into the river.

"What do you think? Shall we try it? On three—one, two... *threeeee*." Freddy yelled as he and Seymour tumbled over the edge.

Seymour came to the surface. "That was great let's do it again."

"Maybe we can later, but first, we need to get someone's attention to ask about Tanks."

The frogs sunk down and floated under the water at a safe distance from the river. *Where are all the fish?* Freddy wondered. At last, one came along. It was a massive fish with a mouth just as big.

"Excuse me, do you know Tanks?" Freddy asked.

The fish gave Freddy the eye, then with a gruff gurgle said, "You talkin' to me? Do I look like I know a Tanks? Don't you know who I am? You can't come around here and ask me questions. I don't have time to talk to the likes of you." He turned and swam away.

"Well," Freddy sputtered. "He wasn't friendly at all!"

A few minutes later, a school of fish came swimming by. "Maybe these are Tanks friends. Excuse me, does Tanks live with you?" Freddy asked.

Back and forth, they shifted as one body. First turning one way then flipping around swimming the other way.

"Tanks?" They turned around. "Tanks who?" flipping back again. "We don't know, Tanks." With each question, they'd switch again. Back and forth, back and forth, making Freddy dizzy. "Why do you think we'd know Tanks? Do we look as if we know a Tanks? We've never heard of a Tanks."

Seymour croaked with laughter as he watched Freddy trying to talk to the school.

"Okay, okay, I apologize for bothering you," Freddy groaned, settling onto the floor of the inlet and shaking his head.

"Oh, no bother, have a nice day," the school said as they swam off.

"What are you laughing at?" Freddy asked as they surfaced to take a breath. He shook his head again.

"You must admit, it was funny," Seymour said, grinning.

"Maybe to you."

As yet nobody knew Tanks.

"Let's try one more time. If no one helps us, we'll head home and hope Tanks comes for a visit," Seymour said as he covered his mouth when another croaking laugh tried to escape. Freddy gave Seymour the look and then sunk back under.

I hope the next group isn't like the last. They made me cross-eyed, Freddy thought as he watched the river.

Freddy didn't need to wait long for another school of fish to come by. One last time he asked, "Excuse me, is Tanks a friend of yours?"

Two fish split off from the group and came over to the two frogs. One fish asked, "Are you Freddy and Seymour?"

"Yes, we are!" Freddy exclaimed. "How did you know?"

Seymour just shook his head. *Sometimes I wonder.*

One fish replied, "We live with Tanks. He's told us about you and the pond."

"Oh, yeah—right." Freddy glanced at Seymour, who was smirking. "We haven't seen Tanks in a while and decided we'd come visiting."

"Could you tell him we're here?" Seymour asked.

"Sure thing, we're just heading home. We'll send him right away," the fish replied. The two fish joined the rest of the school and headed upstream to inform Tanks he had visitors.

While waiting for him, Freddy and Seymour climbed out and rolled over the waterfall again. They croaked with laughter. It wasn't long until their friend swam into the little inlet and tail slapped the two frogs as he slipped in between them.

"It's good to see you," he said.

"Yeah, we thought we'd surprise you, though we didn't plan it very well. We had trouble finding someone to give you a message. Before we leave, we need to figure out a way to let you know we're here without having to ask every fish who swims by," Freddy said while Seymour grinned.

"How's everyone at the pond?" Tanks asked.

Freddy and Seymour caught Tanks up with all the comings and doings at the pond. They told him about Mr. 'gator and Bruno.

Freddy gazed up at the sun. "It's time we head back. Can you think of an easier way to contact you on our next visit?"

Tanks thought for a moment then replied, "Well, I live in the cave where my rock is. Maybe you could dangle a stick into the hole."

"That won't work because sticks could fall in anytime," Seymour explained. "We need something different—I got it. We can borrow a bit of string from Makula. She has several bright colored ones. Honey can tie knots, maybe she can tie a rock on the end. It'll be different and then you can meet us here at this cove."

"That's a great idea," Freddy said. "What do you think, Tanks?"

"I think you came up with the perfect plan, Seymour."

The frogs said goodbye and hopped out of the water by the cove. They found a shorter path to Tank's viewing hole and from there it was a nice lazy hop home. If Freddy and Seymour knew what was happening back at the pond, they'd have been hopping faster than flickin' a fly to get there.

Chapter 14

Toady, tucked away inside his log home, croaked with laughter as he watched the uproar. *It's about time the disgusting creatures get what they deserve for how they've treated me. About time, they learn their lesson.* He slid deeper into the log. *This entire area will be all mine. No one will be around to tell me what to do.*

When Freddy and Seymour arrived back at the pond, they came into the middle of a wild flurry of turmoil. Everyone in the water was swimming in circles, all the birds were flipping and swirling in the air, and the squirrels were chittering as they raced back and forth on the bank.

The two frogs stared in amazement. Their friends had gone crazy. What could cause such a ruckus? Nobody paid any attention to the two frogs sitting on the edge of the pond, except James. He crawled over to Freddy. "This is terrible. Did you see it?"

"What's terrible? See what? We just came back from visiting Tanks. What's happened?" Freddy asked.

Freddy looked around, noticing the owl wasn't there. "And where's Watcher?"

"He hasn't been around, though that's not the problem. Peanut caught the scent and identified it as a bobcat. He was at the edge of the Old Forest." James said as his shell gave a little shudder.

"What's a bobcat? Is it like a wolf?" Freddy asked.

"I don't know, it's what Peanut called it. He said they're fierce fighters and the only safe place is in the water."

Freddy and Seymour had to find out more. They leaped into the pond and swam over to Honey, who was herding her little ones toward the lodge.

"We're back from visiting Tanks. What's a bobcat?" Freddy asked.

"Glad you're home—can't talk now—need to move the kits inside. Ask Peanut, he'll explain everything."

The frogs changed course and headed toward the dam. Peanut stood on top, facing the Old Forest.

"Peanut," Freddy croaked. "We've just come back from Tanks

place. Why is everyone all worked up? What's causing it?"

Gone was the scent of the big cat, even though Peanut sniffed the air, trying to catch it. He glanced down for a moment at Freddy and Seymour. "I caught the scent of a bobcat and Romero observed him on the edge of the Old Forest." Peanut stood back up and sniffed. He continued, "We don't know if he's still around, so we're taking steps to be safe. Honey's moving the kits into the lodge. Since bobcats can climb trees, Makula and Romero are searching for places in the lofty branches where they can stay while we watch if this cat comes back."

"What about Ziggy and the squirrel crew? Are they safe?" Seymour asked.

"Yes. They've holes they can retreat to and the bobcat can't reach them. The problem is we can't live stuck in our lodges or up on top branches. We need to gather food and later get ready for winter. We can't allow this bobcat to stick around."

"Where's Watcher?" Freddy asked.

"Can't say. I saw him fly into the Old Forest this morning, though I'm not sure if he has returned," Peanut replied.

This isn't good, not good at all. "Let's head over to the owls' tree," Freddy suggested. "Maybe he's there and we can ask him what we should do."

"What? Leave the water and hop over to his tree?"

"Take a canal," Peanut suggested. "The second one goes right by it."

Freddy and Seymour found the canal and headed toward Watcher's home. It wasn't normal for him to stay away like this.

Seymour and Freddy reached his tree. While still in the canal, they noticed two things. He sat with his back against the trunk and his left wing drooped with dark stains on his feathers.

"You're hurt!" Freddy exclaimed as he jumped out of the water.

Seymour followed Freddy, though he kept twisting his head about, scanning the area for the bobcat.

"I will be fine; it is just a few pulled feathers."

It appears worse than pulled feathers to me. "How did it happen?" Freddy asked.

"As I perched on a branch overlooking the alligator's pool and not paying attention to my surroundings, a bobcat reached out and snagged my wing. His claws caught a few feathers and strained my wing. It was a hard journey to reach my home. I do not see myself able to fly for several days."

"Did you know the bobcat's been at the edge of the Old Forest?"

The owl sunk lower on the branch and sighed. "No. I had hoped it would not follow me here."

"I don't believe that's what happened. I think came across our pond and is studying it. Peanut has smelled no fresh scent while he's been on watch. Everyone is doing what they can to be safe."

"I will keep an eye out too, although I will not be of much help for a few days."

"We need to head back to the pond, Freddy, and let everyone know what happened to Watcher," Seymour croaked.

They leaped into the canal and swam home. As they entered the pond, they saw Peanut still standing on top of the dam facing the Old Forest.

Seymour swam up beside the dam. "Smell anything, Peanut?"

"No nothing, still it doesn't mean he isn't in there. Did you find the owl?"

Freddy told Peanut what had happened to him.

"Those bobcats are devious. We must keep an eye out. Romero said he and Makula would keep watch from the treetops. The chicks aren't happy being cooped up on a high branch, however Makula laid the fear in them. She said, 'if you think this is being cooped up, I'll put you in a cage like your Papá and I had been in.' That quieted them a bit," Peanut chuffed.

To everyone's amazement, Bruno let out a loud warning screech. There stood the bobcat at the edge of the Old Forest. Peanut jumped into the water. Catching the movement, the cat slunk out of the trees and headed straight for the dam. As he drew closer, his whiskers twitched as his nose took in their scent.

JoJo swam up next to Seymour. "What in fightin' slugs is that critter? I ain't seen nothin' like it."

"It's a bobcat and we're in trouble," Seymour said.

Peanut watched as the bobcat sniffed at the dam. *We can't let him cross over.* With a quick idea, Peanut whacked his tail on the water. The loud smack echoed off the trees around the pond, startling the cat. He spun around to catch what made the noise while Peanut slipped closer to the bank.

He forgot the dam and silently padded to where Peanut tread water. Freddy and Seymour held their breath as the bobcat approached him.

"Come on a little closer," Peanut whispered. He pulled his tail under the water and waited. The big cat leaned forward snorted, then whoosh; Peanut flicked a tail full of water straight into his face.

The cat jumped back and hissed. He shook his head and loped toward to the Old Forest. He stopped at the edge and glanced back at the pond. He drew his lips back, snarled, then swung around to enter the forest.

"That was close, but what caused him to leave so fast?" Freddy asked.

"Bobcats hate getting wet. We're safe for the moment, still we need to figure out how to chase him away for good," Peanut replied.

For the rest of the afternoon, the group discussed ways to drive the cat from their pond. JoJo was remembering about his son's rescue a while back. "To bad we ain't got quicksand, because we could set a trap, so it don't get on the dam."

Peanut stopped his circling. Everyone waited for him to speak. He looked at the group, "I'll be right back. I need to ask Honey a question." Peanut took off for the lodge, while JoJo, Seymour and Freddy waited.

Peanut swam back to the group. "Honey agreed with my plan about the dam. If it works, then this side of the pond will be safe."

"So, what's yer plan?" JoJo asked.

"Well, you got me to thinking when you talked about quicksand…"

JoJo interrupted, "But we ain't got no quicksand."

"True, though when you said, 'to set a trap', it sparked a memory. I've witnessed humans making traps, and we can too. It needs to be wide and deep. Wide enough he can't jump over and land on the dam, and deep enough he can't leap out of the hole."

"Well, he ain't stupid, I reckon. He'd knowd there be a hole," JoJo jested.

"Not if we place branches on top to hide it."

"Oh, that be right smart thinkin' Mr. Peanut."

Freddy shuddered, "Are we just leaving him in there? I don't want to hear his snarling growls until he dies."

"Hadn't thought of that aspect. I don't want to kill him; I just want him to leave us alone. I need to talk to Honey again." Peanut turned and swam back to his lodge.

"That Honey be right smart about them things, just like my Blossom." JoJo puffed up with pride thinking about his mate.

Peanut came back and told them about his change of plans. "I'll still make it the same way, except Honey suggested a ramp. If I do that, then the cat can leave, still he won't be able to cross to the other side of the pond."

"Sounds good, but how will you keep this a surprise? He'll see you digging," Freddy asked.

"I've a plan for that too." Peanut hollered for Romero to come to the pond. When Romero arrived, Peanut swam over to the safe side of the pond, explained the plan and asked, "Will you keep watch while I dig? Give me a warning if you spot him."

"Sí, I watch."

JoJo swam home to tell Blossom about Peanut's plan. *Yep, that Peanut's one right smart beaver and so's his mate. I'm surely glad we got us some good friends.*

Toady watched as Peanut began digging. *Wish I knew what he's doing.* "Can't ask either. I've fooled them this far into thinking I understand everything," he mumbled to himself. "Wait until the beast comes crawling up the grubber's tree. She's going to get what she deserves." Toady croaked and smacked his lips with anticipation.

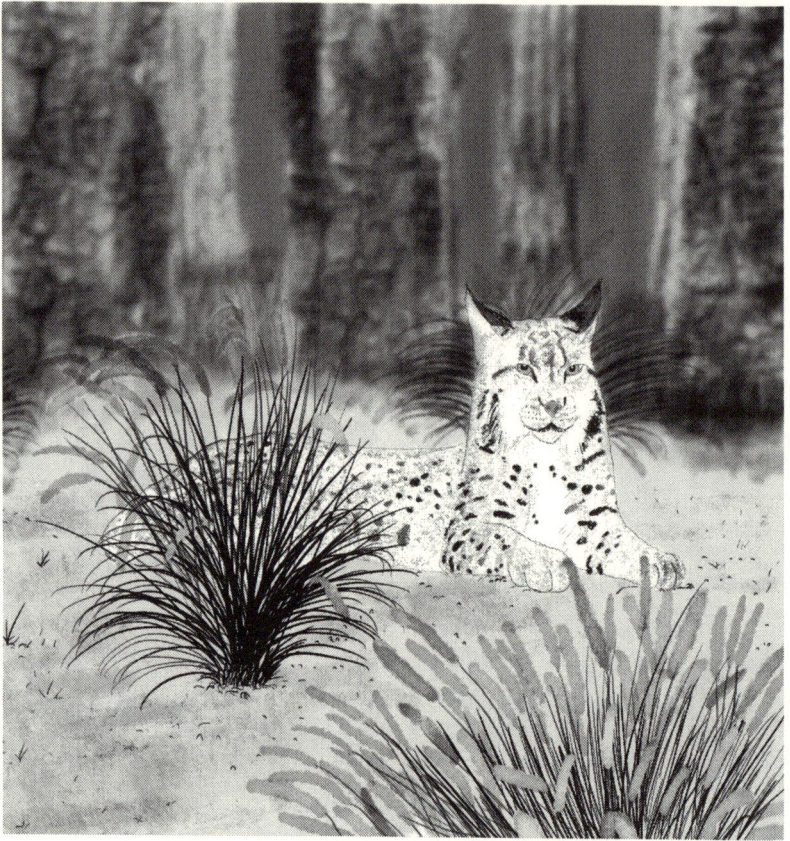

Chapter 15

It took Peanut half of the day to scoop out a shallow hole. He was lucky boulders weren't a problem where he was excavating. He took a minute to check his work and decided it needed to be a little wider. "One chance, that's all I'll get," he mumbled. "Can't make a mistake or it'd be bad for my friends. The question is how to do this quick enough for it to stay a surprise."

He returned to digging, and Romero kept watch for any sign of the bobcat. Since this task would be a long one, Bruno and Mateo took their shifts while their father searched for food.

Honey came out of the lodge and swam over to where the frogs were watching the excavation. "Can you stay with the kits? I want to help Peanut dig. The faster we finish this, the better it will be for all of us."

"Sure thing. I wish we could do more to help," Freddy croaked.

"Just entertaining the kits is plenty. Thank you." Honey climbed out of the pond, waddled over to the hole, and called down to Peanut, "Could you use an extra pair of paws?"

He gave her a toothy grin. "I was wondering how I'd get this done by myself."

"What do you want me to do?"

"It would help if you would get rid of the dirt. I don't want the cat to notice what we're up to. Be careful and keep an ear out for Romero's warning."

Freddy and Seymour swam off toward the lodge. Bucky stuck his head out and saw them coming.

"Can we come out now, Uncle Freddy?" Bucky asked.

"No, your maw wants us to stay inside."

He ducked his head and whacked the water with his tail. "No fair. Our friends get to stay out there and watch. Why does Maw treat us as if we were babies?"

"It won't be for long. Come on, let me tell you about the time Seymour and I…"

The bobcat didn't show up again for the rest of the day. Though exhausted with the constant worry the cat would make an appearance or his excavating wasn't fast enough, Peanut kept on working.

At sunset, everyone found a safe place to sleep. Freddy and Seymour headed for the Grandroom of their cave. Protected in their lodges, JoJo and the beavers stayed safe while the turtles tucked into the frog's old cave and out of the reach of the bobcat. The squirrel crew huddled in their holes. Makula and her family had it the worst. They had to find places in the top branches and couldn't return to their nest. Everyone hoped by the end of the next day Peanut would finish the trap.

Though tired, the beaver's mind zipped along, dreaming about the trap...

Down, down, deep at the bottom of the pit, he dug at a feverish pitch. His claws ached and his arms trembled as his strength melted away. The full moon lit the top of the walls, yet the corners were as black as night. The silent bobcat crept up on the unsuspecting beaver...

Peanut shook himself awake.

Honey rolled over, "Are you okay?"

"Yes, just a bad dream. I guess I might as well get back to digging. I don't think I'll be able to go back to sleep."

Peanut worked hard all day while Honey continued to remove dirt. She pushed it into the river on the other side of the dam and the water swept it away. Romero, Bruno, and Mateo continued to watch for any sign of the bobcat.

Romero chattered to his two sons. "We go to Old Forest. Maybe we see cat before he comes out. This give Peanut much better warning."

His chicks agreed. The one on watch would fly to a tree on the edge of the forest.

Freddy and Seymour stayed with the kits, telling stories. It surprised them on how many they had collected from their journeys. The kits listened and the parts involving them they joined in, but what they wanted to do most of all was play outside.

Honey stuck her head up through the doorway and Bucky whined, "Maw, please, can we go out and play now? I'm tired of staying inside."

"Go ahead, but just a quick swim then come back in to eat. I need to get your Paw something too."

The frogs used this break to look in on the owl. He seemed better today, except his wing still drooped.

"Can you explain what Peanut is doing? I do not have an unobstructed view from here."

They told him about the hole.

"He's making a ramp too, that way the cat can escape out of the hole. I think it would be horrible to listen to his screams while he died a slow death in the pit. We just want him to leave," Freddy croaked.

"I have noticed the humans doing the same thing, except they do not make a ramp. They wanted to capture the animal, not let him go. Maybe he has already left."

"No, he's still around. I've heard him growl and snarl in the Old Forest," Freddy complained. "It echoed all over the place."

"Is there anyone watching the forest?"

"Romero and his sons are taking turns. Seymour and I are watching the kits while Honey helps Peanut. She wants it done now. Speaking of the kits, we should head back. Hope you feel better really quick. We miss you at the pond."

As Freddy and Seymour headed toward the canal, Ziggy eyed the two frogs and glided off the limb to talk to them.

"We don't have a clue in what's been happening, since we're stuck in our holes."

Freddy again explained what Peanut was working on. Excited with the chance they might come out soon, Ziggy jumped onto one of his friend's trees, and skittered up to spread the word.

"Before we head back to the kits, let's check the hole." Seymour said. They swam over to the other bank and took a quick look around. With the bobcat nowhere in sight, they climbed out of the pond.

Peanut was at the bottom.

"This sure is deep. How much more do you need to dig?" Freddy asked.

"I'm almost done with it. I still need to drag the branches over to place on top. Since there is nothing below to hold them up the placement is critical."

At that moment, a screech came from the Old Forest.

"Quick—get in the pond," Peanut said as he scampered out of the hole. He and the two frogs leaped into the water, waiting to see if the bobcat was heading their way.

Romero swooped down, "Bobcat stay at border of forest. He is watching."

"Did he spot me working on the hole?" Peanut asked.

"No," replied Romero. "I gave warning early, you out quick."

"Good. It's still a secret, though it also means I can't dig until he leaves. I'll go explain to Honey, then head out to gather the branches I must cover the hole. As long as the bobcat doesn't come by, it'll stay a surprise."

Peanut took off and Romero flew back to where he left his sons. He didn't want to leave the two chicks by themselves for long.

As Romero settled next to Bruno he asked, "Anything new happen?"

"No," Bruno said. "He's been laying there. His tail is twitching a lot, that's all."

"Thank you, Bruno, and you too, Mateo, for helping with watching," Romero said. "I am very proud of you both."

Bruno's chest puffed out with happiness. He hoped to erase the terrible mistake he made with the alligator. The praise from his father made Mateo, happy knowing that he was pleased with him.

Chapter 16

For the rest of the day the bobcat lay inside the forest line, keeping an eye on the pond. He didn't realize he, too, was being watched. He thought if he stayed in the cover of the trees, no one would notice.

At sunset, the bobcat stood and stretched. He softly padded away from his spot and strolled deeper into the forest. He needed to hunt.

Romero and his two chicks flew back home first stopping to report to Peanut. "The bobcat has left to travel deeper in forest."

"Thank you. I'm tired, yet I feel the need to finish this now instead of waiting for morning."

Peanut gathered the branches he'd cut earlier that day and dragged them over to the hole. He worked through the night, finished the job just before sunrise, then swam home to sleep.

No sooner did Peanut lay his head down than a terrible scream broke the silence. He jumped up and ducked out of his lodge to find out what happened.

Romero came swooping over to Peanut. "It worked! Bobcat came early, wanted to sneak across dam, but fell in hole."

Just then, Peanut saw the cat scamper out of the trap. He growled at Peanut and Peanut yelled back, "Leave now! There's no way over the dam. You'll never cross to the other side of the water."

The bobcat snarled in anger for being outsmarted by a beaver. The cat padded back to the hole, looked at the dam and saw it was too far to jump. He might slip into the nasty water he hated. The bobcat screamed again and turned toward the Old Forest, then paused. Hunger pains gnawed at his insides. The small mouse he'd caught wasn't enough. Big game was scarce because of the fire. Once more, he looked back at the dam then drifted downstream.

The outcry had brought everyone to the pond; even Watcher showed up, though his movements were slow. The only one missing was Toady. The community watched as the big cat left their area.

Toady was mad. He had been dreaming of having his land to himself again. He beat his hands against the wall of his hole. *Stupid beaver had to ruin my plans of a peaceful place. He had better stay in the pond or I'll make him pay.*

The group erupted with praise for a job well done. Their pond was safe again, thanks to Peanut's hard work.

Toady climbed out of his hole and croaked, "Shut up!" But no one paid any attention to him. He crawled around behind his rock and thought about revenge.

Freddy looked for Peanut to thank him, but he wasn't around. He had watched the bobcat drift downstream, then swam back to his lodge for some well-deserved sleep. It had been a long night.

The sun rose higher from behind the mountains as Freddy and Seymour plopped onto their favorite lily pads. They chose the ones with purple flowers which shaded them when the sun grew hotter. Because the bugs were making early morning rounds, the two frogs enjoyed a hearty breakfast of gnats and water striders.

Yum these are the best, Freddy thought as he flicked another one into his mouth.

While eating, the two frogs watched Marina, the youngest chick, follow a butterfly. She twisted, twirled, and circled around. She wasn't chasing it as much as dancing with it. The butterfly didn't mind, in fact it played along with Marina.

Marina was the most graceful flier of the three chicks. She loved imitating the many butterflies among the wild flowers. It was like watching sunlight dance and shimmer on the water. With her wings spread out about her, Marina twirled around and around, moving so fast it reminded Freddy of the beautiful colors that came after a rain shower.

"You know something, Seymour? I'll never tire from watching Marina."

"Me either, I love the way the colors of her feathers change as she loops around."

She spun and danced her way to where Toady was lying on his rock. She hovered over him and asked, "What are you doing?"

Toady opened one eye, then flicked his tongue at her. With a graceful move, she lifted away as the tongue fell short of its target.

"Why did you do that?" she asked.

"Didn't you get the message? Come a little closer and I'll show you again," Toady replied with a smack of his lips.

Marina twirled around and drew closer. Toady flicked his tongue and again Marina side swept away. "That's fun let's do it again, except this time I'll try to tap you with my beak."

"Listen, you little grubber, this isn't a game. If I get my tongue on you, I'll pull a few of your pretty feathers out. I'm sure it will hurt. You better just fly away and leave me alone."

"You look sad though, and I was wondering if I could be your friend," Marina said.

"I don't need you or anyone else. Now leave me alone!"

Freddy and Seymour wondered what Marina was doing over by Toady's rock; but didn't dwell on it when Makula skaawed. Marina flipped around and headed home.

"I guess it's nest building time again," Freddy said. "Remember when Marina had a huge twig in her beak and she almost didn't make it up to the tree?"

Seymour croaked a laugh, "Yeah, and Makula took the twig and dropped it back to the ground, suggesting it was too big."

"The ground under the tree is littered with twigs and things which didn't fit," Freddy laughed. "I wonder how the turtles are managing with those sticks dropping on them."

Sometimes Marina's imagination made this lesson tough on Makula, except Makula never lost her temper. Marina wanted a nest that reached from her branch to the one above.

Makula had told Freddy and Seymour the other day, 'There are days, after I have advised Marina, for the hundredth time, that a certain twig won't work, I want to pull my feathers out. She has big ideas and all I want is for her nest to be practical and weather proof.'

On the other side of the pond, Peanut was teaching Bucky the right way to inspect the dam. He showed him how to repair certain little holes while leaving others for the river to flow through.

Freddy saw James, the turtle approaching and figured he would meet him halfway.

"What's up, James?"

"Ziggy's been visiting, and he wants to see you. I said I'd come and fetch you."

"Thanks, I'll swim back with you."

Freddy yelled to Seymour, "Hey Ziggy wants to see us."

"Be there in a splash." With a gigantic leap, Seymour landed close to Freddy, causing the water to push James further away from them.

"Sorry about that James, I didn't mean to do it so hard."

"That's okay, it was fun."

The three of them swam toward Turtle Pond. Freddy noticed the cattails were filling in along the bank. "Are those cattails making it hard to come over to the bigger pond?"

"No, we like them this way. We can still glide through them and besides, it feels cozy on the other side," James said.

"I understand what you mean," Freddy said as they shifted through them.

Ziggy stood by the edge, swishing his tail back and forth.

"Hey, Ziggy, what are you excited about?"

"I'm finally taking off to visit with my family."

"Sounds great. Are you heading out by yourself?" Freddy asked.

"No, Randall's going with me since he's already traveled that way. You'd figure I was dragging his tail through the mud by just asking him. He was reluctant, but agreed to come."

This surprised the two frogs. They didn't think he would go.

"Since he returned from the last visit, he hasn't been hanging out around the pond. Has the community made him angry?" Freddy asked.

"No, it's not you all, Randall's been mad at Swish and Fluff. I guess they had a problem with him making demands. So, he's sulking and keeping to himself. Nothing has changed with him.

He's still the self-centered squirrel he's always been. To be honest, I don't understand why he came back to the pond."

As Ziggy was talking, Bruno listened from the branch above them. *I want to go too. I bet they wouldn't let me if I asked them.*

"We'll be leaving bright and early tomorrow morning," Ziggy said.

"Enjoy your journey. We'll look forward to hearing about it later," Seymour croaked.

Freddy and Seymour hung around with the turtles for a bit, then headed back to the big pond.

As they swam to their lily pads, Billy Bob joined them.

"Hi ya'll, whatcha doin'?"

"We've been talking to Ziggy. He and Randall are leaving tomorrow to visit his family in another forest. What are you doing?" Seymour asked.

"I be scootin' home, Ma won't be happy if' I'm late for supper," he answered as he passed the frogs' water lilies and kept swimming.

The two frogs climbed up on their pads, and Seymour said, "You know I've been reflecting on how it used to be, just the two of us in the little pond. I can't imagine it being that way again. This is much more fun having all our friends around."

"Except for Toady, I agree. Tell you one thing, there isn't a dull moment around here. Something is always happening."

If Freddy had realized the plans hatching in the head of a little chick, his sleep wouldn't have been deep or peaceful.

Chapter 17

Bruno slipped away from his nest the next morning before the sun rose above the mountains. He waited in a tree close to Randall's place. *This is going to be fun. Wish they'd hurry. I can't wait to see the other forest.*

Ziggy popped out of his hole and scampered to Randall's home. "Are you ready to leave?"

Bruno perked up. *Here we go!*

Randall poked his head out and yawned. "What's the hurry?"

Why isn't Randall excited? Bruno wondered.

"You know I want to get an early start. Let's head out."

Randall shrugged, crawled out of his hole and stretched. "This is precisely why I didn't want to go with you. You're always telling me what to do."

Ziggy rolled his eyes.

They left the pond and skittered deeper into the forest. Bruno followed, though kept his distance. He didn't want them to notice him. *At least I'm not going into the Old Forest and I'm not alone.* Yet Bruno forgot one thing. Nobody knew he had left. He'd be missing—again.

Ziggy was feeling very chipper. It was a beautiful morning to start on their journey. Randall, though, took his time and soon trailed behind.

"Come on Randall, pick up the pace," Ziggy chittered over his shoulder as he launched and glided to another branch. *I will not to start a fight, but he sure is asking for it. Why is he dragging his tail like a snail?*

"I'm coming, what's the big rush?"

As Makula was getting ready to search for breakfast, she noticed Bruno was not in his nest. She asked Romero, "Did you see Bruno leave this morning?"

110

"No. He gone before sun come up."

"Did either of you see him?" Mateo and Marina both shook their heads.

"Well, he's a growing chick, and he's always hungry. He must've left early to search for his meal."

The rest of the family took off upriver to find their morning meal. After reaching their usual spot where they always found the best and juiciest bugs, Makula looked around. She still didn't see him. A tiny sick feeling grew in the pit of her stomach. *I wonder where he is?*

After they ate and flew back home, Makula checked the nest and the surrounding trees, however Bruno was nowhere in the area. She spied Peanut by the dam and flew to ask him if Bruno had flown by.

"No, I've been at the dam all morning and he hasn't come this way," Peanut replied.

Makula then flew to Freddy and Seymour's lily pads. She hovered over them since there was nowhere to land. "Have either of you seen Bruno?"

"No, and we've been laying here all morning."

Now worried, Makula needed to ask Watcher. She flew to the owl's tree; except he wasn't home. When his wing mended, he'd been in and out of the area hunting. Makula flew back home to talk to Romero.

"What are we to do?" She asked Romero.

A tiny voice called up to Makula from below. She peered over her perch and saw one of the turtles on the bank under the tree. She glided down and settled in front of him.

Makula asked, "Are you Peter?"

"Yes, I am."

"I couldn't quite hear what you said."

"I overheard you and Romero talking about Bruno."

"Yes, I'm worried because no one has laid eyes on him."

"I have. I was out early this morning looking at the sky, and listening to the sounds of the new day, when Bruno left his perch. He flew toward the squirrel's home."

"Oh, thank you, Peter, thank you. That's good news. At least we've an idea where to start our search for him."

Romero had been listening from the perch above and he flew to land near the little turtle, "Thank you, little friend."

Makula instructed her two chicks. "We need to find your brother. You two are not to leave the pond area for any reason. If you need anything, you are to ask Uncle Freddy and Uncle Seymour. Do you understand me?" Both nodded. "I'll explain to your uncles before we leave."

Mateo glanced at Marina. "He's in so much trouble. I'm glad it isn't me. I don't like it when Mamá gets mad."

Marina, ruffling her feathers and shook her head. "He's in bigger trouble this time."

Makula and Romero flew over to the bank and called to Freddy. He swam over to meet them.

"Peter saw Bruno leave this morning. He said he headed toward the squirrel's homes. We're heading out to search for him, and we told Mateo and Marina not to leave the pond. If they needed anything, they're to talk with you."

Freddy jumped up onto the bank, "I know where Bruno went. Ziggy was talking yesterday about he and Randall heading to their families' forest. Bruno must've heard us, because Ziggy said they'd be leaving this morning."

"Oh, that chick of mine. He'll make all my feathers fall out before he's old enough to live on his own," Makula screeched.

Freddy shook his head. *That chick's in big, big trouble.*

Toady sat on his rock, smacked his lips as he listened to the grubber. "Pay back couldn't be sweeter for talking to me in that disrespectful tone." His words were just a mumble, yet his smug thoughts lulled him to sleep.

Swish had told Ziggy the best crossing to their clan's home was where the meadow narrowed. So unlike Randall, Ziggy didn't stop until he reached the spot Swish had talked about. The danger still existed, no matter how wide it was. They sat on a limb at the edge of the grassland and could spot their families' forest across the way.

What are they doing? Bruno wondered. The squirrels tilted their heads up, turning one way then the other. *I can see the forest across the meadow. What are they waiting for?*

'Sniff, sniff' Ziggy and Randall smelled the air. There wasn't a hint of danger.

"Are you ready, Randall?"

Randal whipped his tail back and forth. "I hate this part. I don't know why I agreed to come with you."

Ziggy rolled his eyes again. *Complain, complain, complain.* He went on as if he didn't hear him. "I say we glide as far as we can before we land. Then there is less time on the ground."

Randall tapped his paw on the branch. "Fine, let's get this over with."

Ziggy took a deep breath, launched off the branch, and glided away from the tree. Randall jumped right behind him. They landed in the tall grass and the race was on. True to his name, Ziggy zigzagged along the natural pathways between the clumps, not touching any grass as he passed by. The shifting of grass was the same as calling beasts to a feast.

Unknown to the three, Watcher sat on a limb a short distance from the squirrels and Bruno. He observed their cautious movements.

Ziggy and Randall made it to the first tree in the family forest and disappeared from sight. Bruno waited a moment, then flew low right above the tops of the tall grass and landed on the nearest tree. Bruno had been too excited to eat his morning meal, and now his stomach was aching. Checking out his surroundings, he had no idea what was good to eat. *I should've eaten before I left. This all looks strange. I need to go where we always hunt.*

Bruno's sudden reappearance surprised the owl. He watched as the young chick flew toward home.

Just as Watcher was ready to leave, Makula and Romero landed in a tree close to where the group had crossed. As they sat there wondering what their next step was, they heard a hoot behind them.

"I knew Ziggy and Randall were leaving for a visit, and I wanted to protect them as they crossed this meadow," The owl explained. "What I was not expecting was your chick, Bruno. I take it he did not receive your approval?"

"No. Why'd he do such a feather-brained thing? I can't get it in his silly little head how dangerous this is." Makula's wings slumped as she leaned against Romero.

"Well, to ease your mind, I saw Bruno leave the forest and head toward home." Watcher paused a moment, then continued, "I have an idea I would encourage you to consider. With your permission, I can help with this problem. I am willing to show your chick there are perils all around him. Would you allow me to do this?"

Makula looked at Romero. He nodded.

"My plans would include a few journeys, for we realize he enjoys traveling to unknown places. With me, he will be safe. I will teach him how to protect himself from dangerous creatures. These lessons will make him more aware of his surroundings. This way he will always be on the lookout for threats."

Again, Makula looked at Romero. This time Romero spoke. "We are most grateful you do this. It a big worry for us. What you need know, he is stubborn."

"Oh yes, I have observed this willfulness many times. I think with what I can teach him, he will realize this quality trait can also cause him great harm. He is smart. I assume you will want to deal with Bruno first for his actions today, and then he can start his lessons with me."

Makula and Romero thanked him before they left.

Chapter 18

When Bruno arrived home after eating his breakfast, he found a furious mother and father. He hadn't thought ahead concerning what would happen when he returned home. What scared him was how silent they were. They stood for a long time and glared at him.

When he couldn't take it any longer, he fluttered his feathers, sat up straight and boldly attempted to launch into an excuse, "I didn't do anything…"

Romero interrupted, "What? You say you do nothing wrong? Did you tell us where you go? Did you think we not worry? You gone a long time."

Ashamed, he slumped lower and stared at his claws.

Then Makula spoke up. "You don't comprehend how dangerous it is out in the wild. If you had run into trouble, would we have known? No, you didn't think, and that's the problem. You want to do things and travel to other places, yet you haven't learned to use your brain. Well, starting tomorrow, you'll be doing a lot of thinking with Watcher. You'll be staying with him. Now go to your perch and we'll talk in the morning,"

The other two chicks had been listening, and both resembled an owl with their wide-open eyes. They had never heard their mother talk that way.

Romero glanced at Makula. "Let us fly to higher branch to catch cooling breeze. Let Bruno think what he has done."

Bruno considered his actions and found he wasn't proud of them. He had made his parents worry and hadn't given a thought to danger. *Now I'm to stay with Watcher? He's scary.* This got Bruno to worrying, and the excitement of his adventure slipped from his mind.

The next morning, Makula's insides twisted into knots. *What am I doing? How can I send one of my chicks away?* She watched as her family ate, yet she couldn't eat a single grub. After they finished eating, she'd be taking Bruno to the owl's tree.

"Romero, are we doing the right thing?"

"*Sí*. He needs to learn. Watcher will take care of him."

"I understand that part, but will Bruno forgive us?" Makula asked as she glanced at her son.

"*Sí*, in his heart he know he did wrong."

Bruno overheard his parents, but he couldn't understand how they could still send him away. His feathers quaked as his stomach came up to his throat. He pecked at his food, but nothing would go down. *What's the owl going to do with me?*

Makula and Bruno headed to Watcher's tree. He had already hunted and was waiting for them. Quiet and afraid, Bruno didn't have any idea what to expect. The one thing his mother had said which stuck in his brain was he'd be staying with the owl.

"Good morning," Makula said.

"Yes, I agree it is," The owl replied.

Makula studied her son, though no words would come out. She nodded at Bruno, and with a flap of her wings she rose from the branch to return home.

I thought she meant to scare me. She's really leaving me here. Bruno was frightened. Sitting with his head lowered, he didn't make a peep. He took a peek and saw Watcher staring with those big yellow eyes. He glanced away as an icy wave traveled through his body. He slumped even lower on the branch and shuddered. The wonderful sounds of pond life diminished as the pounding of his heart took their place. After what seemed forever, the owl spread his wings.

"Let us go."

Bruno sat straight up. *That's it? Let's go?* He didn't argue though, just lifted off after Watcher. Bruno's wings wobbled as they headed toward the Old Forest. *Please, not Mr. 'gator!* He already had one experience of being too close to those sharp, jagged teeth and snapping jaws. To his relief, the owl flew over the top of the Old Forest and continued toward the mountains.

Bruno couldn't keep quiet any longer. "Watcher? Where are we heading?"

The owl didn't respond. Bruno had never been this far. They came across a forest of blackened, skeletal trees. None had leaves. Many trees had vanished completely, except for stumps in shades of gray. Gone were the thick green bushes and plants which made up a living forest. Looking closer, Bruno saw tiny blades of grass and flowers poking up through the gray stuff, but mostly, the land was lifeless. He'd later learn the gray stuff had once been a tree that fire reduced to ash.

He had yet to witness anything like it. Indeed, he'd been a hatchling when the forest fire came and ate the trees last summer. He called out again, "Watcher? What happened to these trees?"

Again, the owl did not respond.

"I guess he can't hear me," Bruno said aloud to himself.

"I hear you. I am not in the mood to explain right now." As he flew, Watcher remembered how beautiful the forest had been...the burst of fresh growth in the trees and creatures of all kinds making their homes among the sweet berry bushes. Wild flowers of every color growing in the sunny spots where the tree leaves hadn't closed in like a cover.

This had been a living forest, now it was a dead one. He studied the ground and saw the fresh new growth. *It will take many years, but it will come back.*

The owl landed on the branch of a large half-burnt tree. It had been the oldest pine tree in the forest and his favorite place when he was growing up. Bruno landed next to him, and sat quietly, waiting for the owl to speak.

"I apologize for not answering your questions before. I will answer them now. This is the first of several lessons you will learn. You asked about these trees. This was my home until last summer. It was a forest, full of life."

"What happened to it?"

"A terrible lightning storm came and struck many trees. They burst into flames, called the burning. Humans came with water to extinguish them and then the rains arrived, though not in time to save my home."

Bruno inspected the bleak deadness. *This had been his home.*

Several questions swirled around in his head, yet two were most puzzling. "I don't understand what lightning or flames are."

For a moment, the owl had forgotten to whom he had been speaking. Swiveling his head around, he blinked. "But of course, you do not have the knowledge of these things. You do not have the experience to understand these situations, and I am supposed to teach you. First, I will try to explain fire. Fire is something which becomes very hot. As if you are in the sun for a while. Do you know this feeling?"

Bruno nodded.

"Fire is many times hotter. When something grows that hot, it eats what it wants and leaves nothing except ash. Lightning is a hot fire, which comes during a storm. You have not observed this type of storm yet, still I am sure we will have a few before winter comes. Not all lightning in storms causes a fire, if it hits a dry tree it will burn. Flames remind me of the color of your father's wings when he flies. I hope you never see flames."

Bruno shuddered in his mind. He pictured his father flying, and then he thought of his mother. His heart sunk to his stomach. He missed her.

"This fire destroyed my home, taking everything from me; but I now found a new one and wonderful friends who care for one another. Lesson one—take care of your family and friends. Treat them with respect and love, because you can never know, if one day, everything will be taken away from you."

Did he lose someone in the fire? Bruno didn't dare ask. He considered the lesson, but before he could ask questions, Watcher raised his wings and leaped off the branch.

He headed toward the mountains. "Let us go."

Chapter 19

Bruno stretched his wings, lifted off the branch, and followed the owl. Thoughts tumbled through his head. *I know I love my family, yet do I treat them with respect? Not lately. I've left twice without telling them. Do I take care of them? No, they take care of me. I need to ask what I can do to change these things.* For now, he trailed after Watcher.

When they came across a river, Bruno asked, "Is this the river we live next too?"

"No. There are three. They flow from the mountains we are flying toward. My Uncle called the rivers the Three Sisters. They join for a brief time in a lake at the base of the slopes. From the lake, the rivers take different paths to the valley below. There are many stories about the Three Sisters. Maybe someday I will tell you. We are heading to that lake."

As they followed the river, the air grew cooler, and the mountains filled Bruno's vision. He grew up with a view of them, yet he never knew how gigantic they were. They made him feel small, a speck of color against the massive green and brown backdrop.

"How much farther?" Bruno shivered. "It's cold."

"Just a little more."

They came around a bend of the river, and a lake came into view. Gazing up at the mountains, Bruno saw the Three Sisters cascading down as waterfalls dropping hundreds of feet before disappearing behind the trees. As they flew over the lake, Bruno had the chance to study it. The center was a deep color resembling the night sky, and as the water reached the banks, the color grew lighter and lighter until he could spy pebbles of various colors.

Watcher found a tree close by and landed. Bruno settled next to him, shuffling into a sunny spot. A gentle gust of wind made little glittering ripples on the water's surface as it glided across the lake. Reeds growing around the bank, gently waved as the wind passed through them.

"What are we doing here?" Bruno asked.

"Wait—listen."

Bruno closed his eyes, and his first impression was stillness.

That changed over time as tiny noises crept in. The buzzing of bees, the reeds rustling by the lake and twittering of small birds. These sounds became comforting, restful, and soon he grew sleepy. He hadn't slept well the night before and now with the peaceful surroundings, his tired mind needed rest. He relaxed on the limb and dozed off.

Late in the day, a high-pitched whistle echoed around the lake.

Bruno startled awake. "What was that?"

"It is the call of the eagle. This is the subject of the second lesson. The eagle is a danger to you. He is not a threat to me because I am big and a fierce fighter. If you hear its call, you rush your family and yourself into hiding." As the eagle circled the lake, he let out another high-pitched cry, then dove straight down, catching something on the bank.

"Why should I be afraid of him? He lives here by the lake."

"This particular eagle lives here, though others live everywhere. We had one soar over the pond not too long ago. I flew out of my tree and the eagle saw it was my home. He left to hunt elsewhere."

Bruno trembled. *We've been in danger and I didn't realize it.* "We're lucky you watch out for us."

It troubled the owl to hear these words. "You must learn to take care of yourself. I might not always be around when danger comes your way."

"I understand Watcher. I didn't mean it to sound as if it was your duty to take care of us."

As the sun set on the horizon, the owl told Bruno to shift closer to the trunk, "We will resume our lessons tomorrow. I must leave to hunt. You will be safe here." He lifted off the branch and Bruno lost sight of him.

The lessons overwhelmed his mind of all he had learned this far. He wondered what else the owl would teach him. When Bruno realized he wasn't going to eat him, he started to enjoy his time. After a while, his brain shut off, and he fell asleep. He didn't wake when Watcher silently landed next to him.

Even though Bruno had listened to the lesson on the dangers that were all around, it wasn't until he saw the eagle it became real. The pursuit of breakfast was a little unsettling for him. He found himself searching the skies more than pecking for bugs.

When he hunted with his family in the past, he hadn't worried about anything except finding the next bug. Thinking back, he remembered his parents examining their surroundings. They'd eat a bug, then scan the area before looking for another.

Watcher observed Bruno with satisfaction, though it took a while for him to eat his fill. Bruno glanced up and saw the owl observing him.

He must assume I'm a scaredy-chick. Embarrassed, he stabbed a beetle as it crawled out from under a leaf.

"There are a few more lessons to learn here," he said as Bruno flew up to land next to him. "Do you remember when the bobcat came to the pond?"

Bruno's heart race as he nodded. He remembered screeching the warning that the bobcat was coming. It had thrilled him when he had heard the approval from his father.

"Before he came to our pond, he was deep in the Old Forest. While I was checking on the alligator, the bobcat appeared out of nowhere and attacked me."

Bruno shivered, ruffling his feathers. His eyes widened with fear. "How did it happen?"

"I was not paying attention to my surroundings nor listening to the noises around me. If I had been doing that, I would have noticed the forest had gone silent. The silence would have told me a hunter was nearby."

"Last night you fell asleep and did not wake when I returned. It left you wide open for an attack. Yes, you were close to the trunk, and I said you would be safe, for I had not gone far. But when you are alone, it is best to find a tree with a hole where you will be safer than out in the open."

Bruno shrunk lower on the branch.

Noticing his reaction, Watcher knew the lesson had sunk in. He continued, "I was lucky the cat's claws caught just a few feathers. It could have killed me. Therefore, you must always keep a part of your mind listening to the sounds or the absence of them around you. They can save your life."

"Do you remember what your parents did when the bobcat came to our pond?" The owl asked.

Bruno thought for a minute, then he remembered. He stretched his wings out as excitement rushed through him. "We flew to the highest part of the tree, where the branches were very slim."

"Do you understand why they did that?"

Bruno lowered his wings and tilted his head. He reflected for a moment then answered, "No, but I trusted them. They always take care of me."

"They went up as high as they could because the bobcat would be too big for the branches. If he tried to reach them, he would fall to the ground. This plan works for animals who can climb trees. However, you are not always safe on the higher branches of the tree either.

"Considering the eagle, and other flying hunters, you are safer in the deep part of the tree, close to the trunk with lots of leaves or a hole to hide you," he explained.

Humbled, Bruno's shoulders sagged as his head lay on his chest.

"I do not tell you these things to embarrass or shame you. My wish is for you to grow up and protect those you love." The owl figured he had received enough information for now.

"We are finished with this place. We will travel to the forest where Ziggy's family has settled. While we are flying, reflect on these lessons."

Bruno had a question. "What I want to know is how do I care for my family? I already love them. I haven't respected them, though I understand now how to make the change, but what does caring look like?"

The wise owl answered. "Watch what your parents do for you, your brother, and sister. Watch what they do for others at the pond. They are your best teachers in that area."

Chapter 20

After Makula had left Bruno with Watcher, she flew back to her nest. She didn't know when Bruno would come home or how long the peace would last, so they were planning to enjoy it. Not that they didn't love Bruno; they loved him very much. It was the constant uneasiness about his actions which caused the strain on her and Romero.

Mateo, however, struggled on a different level. He loved Bruno, yet he was glad he had left. He was always getting into trouble. His parents worried about his brother, and it seemed as if they were unhappy all the time. This made Mateo feel invisible. *Can't they see I always try to do what's right?*

Marina, his sister, was a show-off. Everyone loved watching her twirl, and glide as she floated like a feather drifting on the wind. He even enjoyed watching her too. Yet being the quiet one, no one seemed to notice him.

I wish Papá would pay attention to me. I don't want to be a troublemaker or a showoff. I just want them to know me for who I am.

What Mateo didn't realize was his parents knew what type of chick he was. Because of all the disturbance Bruno had caused, they just hadn't had the chance to tell him. Now Romero and Makula realized they had been neglecting their other chicks, but this was about to change.

The morning Bruno left, Romero said to Mateo, "Mamá and I need to talk to you."

With what Mateo had been thinking about Bruno, his eyes widened with worry. *Do they know how I feel about Bruno? Did I do something wrong?*

Romero saw the look. "You have done no wrong. We no tell you how happy—no, that is not right word—Makula you say what we want to say to him."

"We are very proud of you. We realize we've been spending a great deal of time with Bruno and you've probably been feeling left out. Even though Papá and I haven't said it out loud, we are aware of your kindness to others. Like the time you helped Bucky with his rock collection. We know you are dependable and we are grateful you watch over your little sister. We love each of you, even during hard times. Thank you for being such a good chick."

Surprised, Mateo stuttered, "I…I—didn't think you knew how I felt—as if you didn't see me. I hope you aren't mad that I'm glad Bruno isn't here."

Romero skaawed, "To be true, it is a break—yes, that is the word. A break for us to no worry about him."

"We figured you felt that way, so Papá decided you and he needed to spend a little time together. He's taking you on an adventure," Makula replied.

"Really? When do we leave? Where are we going?"

"Tomorrow we go," Romero answered.

Marina had been listening, and when she heard her mother talk about the adventure, she screeched, "That's not fair. Why does he get to go all by himself? I want to have an adventure too."

"Mateo needs time with his father. Now you and I can have some fun together," Makula said.

His mother didn't see the anger and unhappiness in Marina's eyes, though Mateo did. He could imagine the thoughts running through her head. *What you think is fun, means work for me.* Mateo laughed to himself.

As the sun set, Mateo squirmed in the nest, plumping his feathers then ruffling them back into place. Excitement raced through him. I wonder where Papá will take me. *I wonder if it will be scary?* At last he settled down and fell asleep only to dream…

Following behind father, we fly toward the Old Forest. The branches click and sway, but there is no wind to cause the movement. Reaching out like claws, the branches pinch together, stretching closer to grab Papá. I need to help him. My wings feel heavy, as if they are carrying a pile of stone and it's taking all my strength to lift them. Something is wrong—I'm afraid to look.

Terrible images fill his mind as he slips deeper into the dream.

I can't lift my wings. I have to look. What's...what's on them? It looks like some kind of black slime covering them? I want to go home, except the trees are blocking my way. They are moving closer, reaching out...

His father trilled quietly in Mateo's ear. "Wake up, it is time we go."

Mateo popped up. The sky was growing lighter. "Papá, we aren't traveling into the Old Forest, are we?"

"No, I do not care for the place."

Romero saw the relief in Mateo's eyes. "You dreaming about it?"

"Yes. It was a scary dream about the trees trying to grab you."

"Do not worry, we head downriver. I take you to where Mamá found me. But no human must see us."

They left after their morning meal and headed downriver. This would be the first time he'd be flying in that direction. His mother had said humans lived there, and he was never to go that way.

Mateo's heart raced, *What are humans? What do they look like?*

Thinking about Marina, he flipped a quick loop in the air. *She was so mad she didn't get to come along.* His wings felt light as he drafted through the soft air.

Mateo's eyes scanned the clear river below him. He saw an assorted variety of fish swimming back and forth. A quick glimpse of a bright color, very much like his Papá's wings, caught his eye.

"Look, is that Tanks swimming around those little fish?"

Romero spotted the fish. "*Sí*, Tanks with friends. He live near here."

Tanks glanced up as the shadows played across the surface of the river. *I wonder where they're going?*

On the two birds flew, farther from home. They came across another river, which joined the one they were following. The trees were different here; they had needle-like leaves. Not too many were the same as his tree at home. Romero turned away from the river and entered the nearby forest.

Romero landed on a branch. "We are close. From here we be quiet and not seen."

Staying in the higher branches, they made small, swift flights between the trees. Each time they stopped, Romero surveyed the ground below and the area around. Mateo grew tense with each stop.

Excitement changed to dread as he remembered his dream. He quickly checked out the trees and saw they weren't moving, though it didn't stop thoughts of danger creeping in. The bush below him rustled. *What's there?* He put all his focus on the bushes and waited for a creature to jump out or a set of glowing eyes to stare back at him. He listened for the clicking of the tree branches…

"We are close enough," Romero whispered.

Mateo jumped and screeched. His imagination had taken a hold of him and he had forgotten he was with his father.

Romero gaped at him as if he had lost his mind. Mateo shrunk lower, with his chest resting on the limb, and didn't look up. "Sorry, Papá, I guess my imagination became too real, and you scared me."

He laughed. "So evil creatures coming for you?"

"Yes, something like that," Mateo also laughed at his own behavior.

"Just there is cabin I lived. Do you see?" Romero pointed to a box made of wood.

A big tree trunk blocked Mateo's view. He crept to the end of the branch. "Yes, I can. What are the strange creatures in front of it? They're moving around. What're they doing?"

"Those are humans. The little ones play like you do with your brother and sister."

"Can we move closer? Please? It's hard for me to get a good look."

"Wait, I go. Do not leave. I come back. If they see you, they catch you and put you in cage."

They couldn't catch me, I'm fast, Mateo thought.

It wasn't long after his father had left that a small human wandered over toward the tree. Curious, Mateo leaned out away from the limb to survey the small human. At the same time, it peered up into the tree at him. It yelled, and the others ran toward him.

What am I to do? Papá told me to stay; I don't want them to catch me. With no other choice, he leaped from the limb, flew up through the branches and above the treetops. He searched for his father and saw him flying toward him.

Romero had heard the humans yell and with a swift shift of his wing he turned back toward his son just as Mateo broke through the treetops. He glanced down and saw them running between the trees.

He screeched in fright, "What do I do?"

"Fly, fly away from river. No lead home. We no want them to

find it," Romero screeched.

Mateo took off and headed farther from the river. Romero caught up to him. "We go this way then turn toward home."

As they flew, Mateo saw the edge of the forest and a strange sight beyond.

"Papá, what is that?"

"It is where many humans live. Never go there. They put us in cage."

Mateo's wings wobbled with fear at the thought. Danger was too close here. He'd never come this way again. It was good being on a journey with his father, but he was ready to head home.

"I want to go home."

Romero skaawed, "*Si*, I too want to go home."

They made it back just as the sun was setting. It had been a long day and Mateo would reflect on it often. He had fun; he had adventure—well, at least with his imagination—and he had a small amount of danger.

"Mamá, I don't understand why Freddy and Seymour want to leave on so many adventures. I've had one, and that's enough for me. I'm glad to be home," Mateo skaawed.

Makula laughed, "Yes, those two enjoy their adventures, though they're always glad to come back to the pond."

Mateo asked his mother what she and Marina did. Makula laughed again. "I will let her tell you all about it."

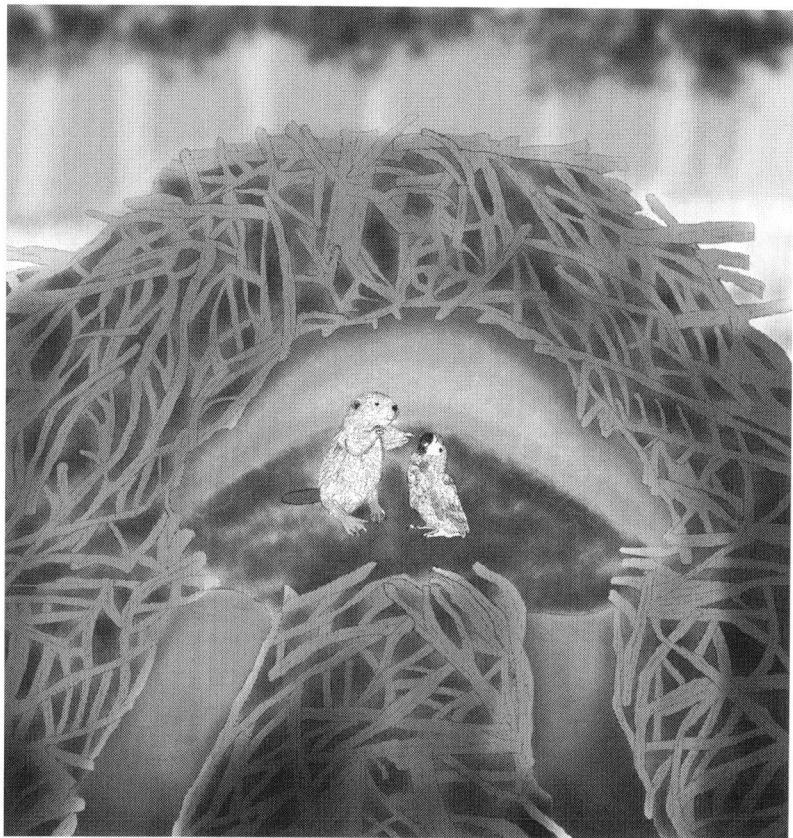

Chapter 21

It had upset Marina about her brother Mateo leaving on an adventure with their father. *Why are my brothers allowed to have these adventures and I can't!*

It also upset her because her mother's idea of fun—wasn't the same as Marina's. To her, fun was playing with the butterflies, gliding games with Swish and Fluff, or picking berries with Strawberry and Joleen. Her mother's idea of fun wasn't fun at all. It was work, or so Marina thought.

Marina plotted a scheme of her own and put her plan into action that night.

"Papá, Strawberry invited me to play at her lodge tomorrow, may I go?"

"Does not your mother have plans? You ask her."

Oh, beetle bug juice. That didn't work like I figured. I must think of something else.

Before anyone was up, Marina flew to Strawberry's lodge to hide on top. She was hungry, though she didn't dare check for something to eat. Strawberry had told her when her maw and paw left, she'd help Marina into the lodge.

After Romero and Mateo departed for their adventure, Makula looked around for Marina. She wanted to get busy with her plans for the day, and Marina had missed breakfast.

"Marina," chattered Makula. "Time to wake up! You're very lazy this morning."

Marina did not answer. *Now where can she be, she knows we're spending the day together.* She took off from the nest in search of her chick.

As soon as Peanut and Honey left to find their morning snack, Strawberry smuggled Marina into the lodge.

"After my Mamá grows tired of trying to find me, we can leave and pick berries."

Marina hadn't realized her mother wouldn't stop looking for her, in fact she'd ask the whole neighborhood to search for her.

It seemed like hours, and Marina's stomach ached. She wasn't used to missing breakfast, and she needed to eat. "Strawberry, maybe it's been long enough, let's go pick berries."

Before they could leave the lodge, Peanut popped up through the door opening and saw Marina. Peanut frowned.

"Marina, you need to come out right now and Strawberry, you go to your room until I come back."

Uh oh, he sure doesn't sound happy. I hope she didn't do anything too bad. Marina didn't have a clue it was because of her that Strawberry was in trouble.

Ducking out of the lodge, Marina flew to the top to shake the water off her wings. She stopped in mid-shake as she looked around and saw the entire neighborhood staring at her. Even sleepy eye JoJo was there. Makula flew to perch next to her and gave her the coldest glare she had ever witnessed. *Oh, beetle bug juice, Mamá is angry.*

"All of our friends have been searching for you. Tell them you're sorry for causing a problem, then go straight to the nest. I'll be there in a minute."

Ducking her head with embarrassment, Marina mumbled, "I'm sorry for causing you this much trouble." Then she flew straight to the nest because when mother was that mad, you did what she told you to do.

Makula looked down at her neighbors from her perch on the beaver's lodge, "I apologize for my chicks. I know Bruno has been a stubborn bird, however I didn't expect this behavior from Marina. I'm sorry for them being bothersome. Thank you for helping me search." Saying this, Makula tucked her head in embarrassment and headed toward the nest to deal with Marina.

As Makula landed on her limb. Toady croaked at her, "Well, your chicks are becoming fine little trouble makers, aren't they? First, you had to send one away now this little show off isn't so delightful is she."

"Stuff your tongue back in your mouth, Toady."

"I will not! I can say whatever I please and I wouldn't allow a toad to behave that way," he answered back.

"Your actions are just as bad. Did your clan kick you out before you had training in manners? At least my chicks are teachable whereas you are too ignorant to learn."

"Chrip-it." Toady fumed as he slid off his rock and crawled underneath. *She knows nothing about my clan. I'm happy she's getting what she deserves.* Even with these words, he didn't feel satisfied as his anger boiled inside him.

Marina knew she was in big trouble. She huddled in the hollow part of the tree, and in a miserable state of mind. *Will Mamá send me away with Watcher, never to return home?*

Makula stepped along the limb to settle next to her daughter. "You made a terrible decision to hide from me. What were you thinking? You aren't willful as your brother Bruno. In fact, everyone loves your sweet, caring heart. Why would you want me to worry?"

Marina glanced up at her mother. "I didn't consider that, I guess I wasn't using my brain at all. I just wanted to have fun and not do the things you had planned. I hadn't meant for you to worry. I'm sorry."

Makula tilted her head, looking at Marina. *Have I forgotten how to have fun?* "What do you enjoy doing for fun?"

Marina peered up at her mother. "Well, I like the gliding games Ziggy and the crew compete in and picking berries and—you know—play."

"That's interesting, because my plans had included berry picking and a small trip up the river to gather a few rather tasty seeds you love to snack on. But instead you caused me to waste mine and the neighbor's time searching for you, so for the rest of the day you'll repay our friends for their kindness in helping me. You'll gather berries for the beavers, collect nuts for Ziggy and the crew, and find a few juicy bugs for JoJo, Freddy and Seymour."

It became apparent to Marina how much trouble she had caused. She didn't want to be like Bruno, and now she was embarrassed to have acted the same way with her selfishness.

"But Mamá, I said I was sorry. Do I have to do those things?"

"Yes, you do. This will show our neighbors you are feeling bad for causing trouble, and it will go a long way in proving it to them."

Marina left the nest, taking the little hauler her father had made. A butterfly came by to dance, but she kept flying. Her heart hurt and she felt miserable. *I really messed up and I need to apologize to Strawberry. Hope she won't be mad at me for getting her in trouble.* Settling by the berry bush, Marina picked a big juicy berry and plopped it in the hauler. *I hope the others will forgive me too. I need to show my friends I care about them.*

It pleased Makula there hadn't been any more arguments from Marina and she wanted to do the right thing. For Makula it had been a tiring day and not at all what she had planned. She hoped this lesson would teach Marina to think twice before doing something like this again.

Then her thoughts drifted to Bruno. *How is he doing? I hope he stays safe and listens to Watcher, but I miss him and I want him to come home.*

Chapter 22

Watcher and Bruno descended from the lake, following the Saylo River. They flew between towering canyon walls, which opened up to a flood ruined landscape. The scaring left by the fire was different. It had blackened the trees, misshaping and twisting their branches into cruel knots. Here, the flood left big gaping holes from uprooted trees. Shredded limbs and tattered trunks lay everywhere, leaving distorted stumps. Nothing green had escaped the flood or the fire.

"We will not stop here. We must fly to the forest where the squirrel crew's family live. Ziggy and Randall, who are visiting, should still be there. I want to protect them on their journey back to the pond."

When Bruno had followed the squirrels, he had observed no dangers. Now after spending time with the owl it made him aware of many kinds of threats, and they were everywhere.

Bruno asked, "Have you been to the heart of that forest?"

"Yes, I have, and it is another reason we are going there. It is a different forest from all the others. It is ancient. Much older than the Old Forest. When you enter this one you feel a disturbing sense of danger all the time."

Listening to Watcher, Bruno decided he didn't care for this place at all. Bruno's wings wobbled. *I'm tired of being scared.*

"What troubled you?" Bruno asked.

"That is the problem. I have seen nothing. If you can spot it, you can protect yourself from it."

He's just trying to scare me. He wouldn't take me where I'm not safe. Still, Bruno wasn't sure about that either. They flew toward the forest, and the owl glided lower for a better view. At that very moment, a huge bird burst from the top of a tree, and aimed right for them.

"Dive for the trees!" Watcher screeched.

Bruno didn't pause; he folded his wings and shot for the leafy cover. Just as he reached the top branches, he felt the rush of air and the graze of talons from the giant bird.

The young bird shuddered as he landed and shifted closer to the trunk. He pulled in his wings and squeezed them tight to his sides. From his hiding place, he watched the bird attack Watcher. The owl was just as fierce. He swept up and over, clawing at the bird's large eye. Screeching, the giant bird broke off from the attack to find easier prey. Watcher flew to where he saw Bruno enter the forest.

"Bruno, where are you?" The owl hooted.

"I'm here, just a few branches below you."

Surprised, he landed next to him. "You hid yourself very well." Surveying the sky above, he took a deep breath. "That was a close one. You followed instructions without hesitation and you were fast, which saved your life."

"No. You saved my life. I wouldn't have known to dive. I'd have flown around trying to avoid getting caught. What kind of bird was it?"

Watcher considered his answer. "I am not pleased in saying this; for once I do not have any idea."

Bruno double blinked as he stared at the owl. *The Watcher is wise, so for him to say he doesn't know is an unbelievable thought.*

"It will be safer to stay under the shelter of the treetops."

The owl flew through the outer ring of trees and stopped just before they reached the trees where Ziggy's clan lived.

"The big Oak tree there in the middle of the clearing is where they are. Other than Ziggy and Randall, these squirrels do not know me. I do not want to scare them; please find Ziggy and guide him here."

Bruno took off and flew to the little opening amongst the circle of trees. He landed on the ground and waited.

A squirrel popped out from behind a tree. "Do you want something?"

The young bird looked up at the squirrel, "Yes, will you please ask Ziggy to meet with me."

With a twitch of his tail, the squirrel streaked around the tree. Bruno waited, though it wasn't long before the squirrel returned with Ziggy. Randall was close behind.

The two squirrels jumped to the ground and ran over to Bruno, "Hi Bruno, why are you here?"

"I'm with Watcher. He asked me to find you and bring you back to him. He needs to speak with you and didn't want to scare your family."

Ziggy chittered with a laugh. "He definitely would have scared everyone. They probably wouldn't come out of their holes for days."

Bruno lifted off the ground and the two squirrels leapt on to the nearest tree. They followed Bruno and found the owl waiting for them.

"Is there anything wrong back home?" Ziggy asked.

"No, everything is fine there. Have you noticed the giant bird which has taken up residence here?"

"Yes," Ziggy said. "He hasn't come to this outer part of the forest. He stays in the top of the trees near the center. My family says the middle of the forest is dangerous and we aren't to go in there. Have you been there?"

"Yes, I have, and I agree. How long has this bird been here?"

"He came a day after we arrived. To be honest, it worried me on how Randall and I were to get safely across the meadow."

"It was right for you to worry. I do not believe it will be safe to depart without protection. If you like, when you are prepared and ready to leave Bruno and I will fly back with you."

"Thank you, Watcher, we'd be grateful for your protection. We'll be ready to start back in the morning, if that's okay with you," Ziggy replied.

Randall just shrugged. *I've made the trip plenty of times and nothing has happened.*

The shrug annoyed the owl, not because he considered himself to be all-important, but it was because Randall's attitude could mean trouble for Ziggy's safety.

"Yes, it will be fine. Shall we meet again at this tree? We have been away from the pond for a few days and one of us is eager to return home," Watcher said as he glanced at his companion with his large yellow eyes.

The young bird lifted and flapped his wings, thinking of home. "Yes, I'm ready to see my family. It feels like it's been a long time since I've left."

After the squirrels zipped away, the owl flew deeper into the forest. There was a sense that something wasn't right.

"I thought Ziggy said it wasn't safe in here," Bruno whispered. They glided quietly from one tree to another. The two birds settled on a branch and Watcher replied.

"It is unsafe if you are not careful. Listen. What do you hear?"

Bruno glanced around. Nothing stirred. There were no birds singing, no creatures rustling in the bushes, and no wind whispering through the dried leaves.

"I don't hear anything, but my pin feathers are prickly."

"Exactly my point."

The owl ruffled his feathers, took a deep breath and hooted. Bruno twitched and jumped. He turned to stare at Watcher. Suddenly the forest came alive. The scurrying and rustling of startled creatures leapt through the bushes. Birds gave a chirp of warning as they flapped their wings and settled back down. Then the silence returned.

"What was that all about?" Bruno whispered. "I don't understand."

Watcher looked around. "Something keeps them frightened."

"Is it because of the giant bird?" Bruno asked.

"No, I have visited this forest long before the giant bird arrived. When I called out, I got the same results."

"What do you believe has scared them?"

"Again, I have to say, I do not know why. We need to find a creature who can explain it to us."

"Why do they stay? Wouldn't you think they would want to leave?"

"Let us find a creature who will answer those questions."

Finding anything bigger than a mouse who shook with fear at the sight of the owl was harder than they thought. The day was growing to an end.

"I do not want to be here when night comes. This will have to stay a mystery until another time."

Watcher and Bruno left the inner forest and flew to the outer ring. They settled into a more comfortable perch to sleep before their journey home. Bruno was excited to be heading home and couldn't wait to inform his parents of everything. Thinking of the comforts of his nest, he fell asleep.

Chapter 23

Watcher nudged the sleeping young bird and said, "Awake, it is time."

Bruno leaped up and spread his wings out.

"I am leaving to hunt, you need to search for your meal, but stay away from the deeper part of the forest."

"Oh, don't worry. I wouldn't go in there alone for all the bugs in the forest."

While the two birds were finding breakfast, Ziggy and Randall were saying goodbye to their families. They headed toward the meeting place and found Bruno and the owl waiting.

Watcher explained how they were to proceed. "Ziggy, you and Randall are to move at a slow pace into the meadow. Try not to rustle the grasses and stay in the shadows of the bigger plants. We will wait and if the giant bird appears, we will fly out and draw the bird toward us. Bruno, you will break off and flee to the edge of the other forest, while the two of you run as quick as you can. The important thing is to stay hidden for as long as possible."

Bruno's wing muscles tightened as he perched on the edge of the Ancient Forest. It was hard for him to watch his friends creep into the meadow. He scanned the skies, but they were clear. Ziggy and Randall were doing great, staying in the shadows. In fact, they had disappeared. The grasses swayed as the breeze ruffled the strands.

Suddenly Randall took off at a dead run. The grasses shook and wildly thrashed about him as he ran through them. Ziggy barked at him, but Randall didn't slow down. He couldn't afford to trail behind his wild scamper. The anger boiling inside Ziggy triggered his muscles to run faster than he had ever run before. The giant bird exploded from the top of the trees.

"Fly now, Bruno! I will be there with you."

Bruno leapt from the tree and flew like a crazy bird, dipping and flipping. He dove, then pulled up. He zigged and zagged faster than ever. From above he heard the call of the terrible bird, but he never looked back. A shadow was just above him, so he flipped and headed in the opposite direction. It was too big and couldn't change directions as quick as the smaller bird.

"Turn now, Bruno!" Watcher hooted as he landed on the back of the huge bird's neck, digging his talons in. The bird shrieked with anger, shook his back, and dislodged the owl. Watcher swept sideways as the large beak snapped at him. The owl dove under the bird's belly and scraped its stomach. Another shriek echoed through the air.

Bruno had flipped back again toward the forest. Reaching the trees, he stopped only when he was well under the tree canopy. Bruno scanned the meadow for the two squirrels and saw Ziggy had zipped passed Randall as he raced toward the tree line. The owl's battle screech drew back his attention.

Watcher was swift and clever, even though the huge bird had a long reach. It scared Bruno to watch and do nothing. He wanted to screech and dash out to assist with the fight, yet knew he would just make matters worse for his teacher. The talons of the giant bird stretched out, but the owl was quicker and slid away from the closing claws. Flipping up, he again settled on the back of the bird. Squeezing his talons into the back of the neck, he held on as the enormous bird tried to shake him off again.

Ziggy and Randall sprinted into the trees, and slumped against a tree trunk, too tired to climb up. Their bodies ached from the strain of the long dash to safety.

Bruno let out a loud screech. "They're safe!"

The owl loosened his grip and flew toward Bruno. Breathing heavily, he landed next to the young bird.

He turned to stare at Randall. "You were doing very well why did you run? You placed not just yourself, but also Ziggy and Bruno in terrible danger."

"I figured moving so slow was a senseless idea. I knew I could make it if I ran. Anyway, I didn't ask for anybody's help."

Ziggy's tail bushed out and swished violently back and forth. "No, what you did was stupid and selfish. For as fast as that giant bird was, without Watcher and Bruno's help, you'd be dead. I don't appreciate you trying to get me killed along with you."

"You ran past and left me behind." Randall stomped and whined. Turning his back on them, he plucked a bur off his tail.

With a displeased hoot, the owl realized he would not change Randall's mind. He instead gave Ziggy his full attention. "I am sorry to say this journey is not safe, even with my protection. It was all I could do to keep him from digging his claws into my wings. I will search for a different route to visit your families."

Glancing over at Randall who still hadn't thanked him, Ziggy said, "Thank you Watcher. I'd never have made it without you."

The rest of the journey was uneventful. For Bruno, he wanted nothing more to do with attacking giant birds. Two times was enough. He was more than ready to get home and play with his brother and sister.

The sun was setting when Makula saw Bruno and the owl coming her way. Her heart did a double beat when she saw her chick.

Before she could ask questions, Watcher spoke up. "It has been a long day. We will talk tomorrow."

Romero gave a nod to the owl as he lifted off for home.

Makula eyed her chick. His shoulders slumped from exhaustion. However, she saw something which gave her hope that he had changed.

"Bruno, I'm glad you're home. There'll be plenty of time to

hear about your journey," Makula said.

Romero looked at his chick. "I also am glad you have come home. You seem well. We will talk tomorrow." Bruno nodded his tired head and retreated to his nest in the hollow space of the tree.

The next morning the owl flew to Makula's tree, but before he could share his story, Toady crawled over to the bank and interrupted him.

"I guess my wishes aren't working out as the troublemaker chick is back. Oh well, maybe a solution to my problem will happen next time," Toady croaked.

"Yes, I agree. However, my permanent solution would be to take you to a forest which does not have many creatures living there," Watcher responded.

"I have every right to be here and I have every right to speak my mind."

"Yes, I understand your point. We have the same rights not to listen to your remarks. Therefore, you have a choice. Keep your comments to yourself or I take you on a little—no, a long journey. It might please you to find the solitude you wish for in this other forest."

"Chrip-it!" Toady grumbled as he twisted around and crawled toward his rock. Instead of climbing up on top, he slid underneath. *He doesn't scare me. I'm a toad and I can do what I want.*

Makula came over to perch next to the owl. "Would you really take him away?"

"Yes, I would. Toads are mean and they are stubborn, though not the same as your chick. Bruno is smart and understands what I have been teaching him. Toads, however, do not take instruction from others very well. We have not heard the last from him."

"I can't say I'd be unhappy if Toady left. In fact, he has done a few terrible things, especially to James. Still, I want to think he could change. Am I wrong in hoping for this?"

"I have witnessed some creatures can change. I will watch him."

"Was the journey a success? Did Bruno understand what you were trying to teach him?"

The owl nodded. "It was good for both of us. He taught me a few things too. I have to say, without looking for trouble, we had a few narrow escapes. All these lessons are what he needed to learn. You have a very good and strong son. You should be proud of him."

By that afternoon, everyone at the pond knew Bruno had returned, and they were all excited to call a Gathering to hear of his journey. Watcher, Ziggy, and the crew joined in—except of Randall.

Randall sat by his hole and observed. His tail whipped around with resentment. *I did nothing wrong to deserve Ziggy's treatment. And those other two squirrels are disgusting. They never care about their appearance. I'm better than all of them.* He stomped his foot and leaped back into his hole. He looked around at the tidy home and his anger boiled over. Nuts sailed through the air as he yelled,

"I—don't need—anyone!"

Back at the pond, Peanut asked, "Bruno, will you tell us about your journey?" Bruno tilted his head to look at the owl who blinked and then nodded. Bruno's pinfeathers prickled with excitement as everyone settled comfortably around him. He shook his feathers back into place and began.

He spoke about everything he had observed and the lessons he learned. When he came to the part about the giant bird, everyone shifted to the edge of their perches. Shuddering, Marina slid under her father's wing as she pictured in her mind the battle between Watcher and the huge bird. Billy Bob and Bucky leaned in as Bruno spoke of the enormous bird's talons and how he escaped.

Toady sat under his rock and listened, wondering if the owl's threats were real. *Would he really do it? No, he wouldn't dare. I am a toad after all, and I rule here. But maybe I better lie low for a while.*

Makula folded her wings tight against her body and sat straighter on her perch. As she gazed at her son, she didn't see a chick anymore; she saw a strong and brave young bird.

The End

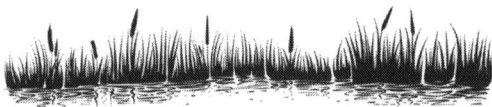

ILLUSTRATOR Faith Jones has been drawing since she was a young girl. Now eighteen, she enjoys a range of mediums, seeking to showcase God's creations with the talent that He has given her. Her favorite places to be are Grace Bible Church, where she is a member, and camping at the beach with her family. Faith is one of 10 children and enjoys reading, crafting, writing, and playing with her nieces.

COVER ARTIST Keith Silvas is an artist and author who has been creating characters and making up stories about them since he was a kid. He lives in Montana with his wife and two cats.

Coming Soon

"Trouble at the Pond"

Book 4 in the series: It Takes a Pond

Bullfrogs JoJo and Blossom go on a journey to visit their kin in Goose Neck Holler. They leave their kids, Billy Bob and Joleen, in the care of Freddy and Seymour.

Wanting to entertain the kids, the two frogs invite the beaver kits, Bucky and Strawberry, to explore one of the canals. That's where trouble strikes.

But it's just the beginning as Peanut comes once again to the rescue in an unfortunate event.

Freddy wonders if things at the pond will ever return to normal.

But what is normal?

Made in the USA
Columbia, SC
28 November 2023